O-gî-mäw-kwě
Mit-i-gwä-kî

O-gî-mäw-kwĕ Mit-i-gwä-kî

Simon Pokagon

MINT EDITIONS

O-gî-mäw-kwĕ Mit-i-gwä-kî was first published in 1899.

This edition published by Mint Editions 2021.

ISBN 9781513283395 | E-ISBN 9781513288413

Published by Mint Editions®

MINT
EDITIONS

minteditionbooks.com

Publishing Director: Jennifer Newens
Design & Production: Rachel Lopez Metzger
Project Manager: Micaela Clark
Typesetting: Westchester Publishing Services

As a token of sincere appreciation, I Pokagon hereby inscribe "Queen of the Woods" to all societies and individuals—benefactors of our race—who have so bravely stood for our rights, while poisoned arrows of bitter prejudice flew thick and fast about them, boldly declaring to all the world that "the white map and the red man are brothers, and that God is the father of all."

The past can never be undone.
The new day brings the rising sun
To light the way of duty now
To children with the dusky brow.

Contents

Preface

The "Queen of the Woods" is a real romance of Indian life by Chief Pokagon. Nearly all the persons mentioned in the narrative bear their real names, and were personally known to many yet living. The reader will bear in mind that in all cases where fictitious names are used, or where the names of persons spoken of are omitted from the narrative, it was purposely done by the author, out of regard for friends and relatives who now occupy the places where certain tragic events occurred. Throughout the whole narrative, the careful reader will note that the author has studiously avoided, as far as consistent, all such acts of seeming cruelty as might tend to increase existing prejudice between the two races. His greatest desire in publishing the historical sketch of his life has been that the white man and the red man might be brought into closer sympathy with each other.

In all his writings he constantly bore in mind the children of this broad land, with the ardent wish that the prejudice against his race, which has been so thoroughly instilled in their young minds by stories told in the home, and taught in the schools through incorrect histories, might in the future be overcome.

"Is not the red man's wigwam home
As dear to him as costly dome?
Is not his loved ones' smile as bright
As the dear ones of the man that's white?

"Freedom—this selfsame freedom you adore—
Bade him defend his violated shore."

A Brief Sketch of Chief Simon Pokagon's Life[1]

His Reception at the World's Columbian Fair at Chicago in 1893

Chief Simon Pokagon was born in the old Pokagon Indian village located on Pokagon Creek about one mile from St. Joseph River, Berrien County, Mich., in 1830. He is a full-blooded Pottawattamie Indian, and the last chief of the Pokagon band. At fourteen years of age he could speak his mother tongue only; he was then sent to the Notre Dame school near South Bend, Ind., where he remained three years. Returning home fired with zeal for a good English education, he succeeded through his own efforts, aided by his mother, in going to Oberlin College, Ohio. Here he remained one year and then went to Twinsburg, in the same State, where he remained two years longer. His father, Leopold Pokagon,[2] was chief for forty-two years, and during

---

1. The names Po-ka-gon and Po-ca-hon-tas are both derived from the Algonquin word Po-ka (a shield or defense).
2. In a history of the removal of the Pottawattamie Indians from northern Indiana, recently published by Daniel McDonald, of Plymouth, Ind., appears the following:—

"The Pokagon Pottawattamie Village, one of the earliest Indian villages in northern Indiana, and where many of the most stirring scenes occurred prior to the removal of the Indians to the Western country provided for them, was located on the line between Indiana and Michigan, north of South Bend and about one mile west of the St. Joseph River.

"Leopold Po-ka-gon, the elder, was the second in rank among the chiefs of his tribe, To-pin-a-be being the first. Pokagon and his people were noted as being the farthest advanced in civilization of all their race in the St. Joseph valley. He has been described as a man of considerable talents, and in his many business transactions with the early settlers was never known to break his word. He set a good example to his followers by not indulging in 'fire water' (whisky). He was particularly distinguished for his devotion to the traditional teachings of the Jesuit Fathers. After the destruction of Fort St. Joseph by the Spaniards in 1781, says Mr. Leeper, in 'Some Early Local Foot Prints,' the St. Joseph Valley was practically abandoned as a missionary field for nearly half a century. Pokagon made several visits to Detroit, especially to ask that the black-gowns (missionaries) be again sent among his people. The last of these appeals was in July, 1830. Detroit was then the residence of M. Gabriel Richard, vicar-general of the bishop of Cincinnati, and to the church official Pokagon poured out the deep yearnings of his soul. 'Father, father,' he exclaimed, 'I come to beg you to send us a black-gown to teach us the word of God. We are ready to give up whisky and all our barbarous customs. Thou dost not send us a black-gown, and thou hast often promised us one. What! Must we live and die

that time, made many important treaties with the United States. He died when Simon, the present chief, was only ten years old.[3] His son, the present chief, was the first red man to visit Abraham Lincoln after taking the presidential chair. His mission was to procure if possible the amount due his people from the sale of Chicago and the surrounding country by his father to the United States thirty years before. Just before Lincoln's death, near the close of the Rebellion, he visited him again. During the year 1866 he succeeded in procuring partial payment of

---

in our ignorance? If thou has no pity on us, take pity on our poor children, who will live as we have lived, in ignorance and vice.' And he went on to recount how his people had preserved the prayers taught their ancestors by the black-gown formerly at St. Joseph; how his wife and children, every night and morning, prayed before the crucifix; how the men, women, and children of his band fasted according to the traditions of their fathers and mothers. M. Frederick Reze was sent temporarily to minister to these urgent spiritual demands. July 22, 1830. he began his work, baptizing Pokagon and his wife as Leopold and Elizabeth respectively; the one at 55 years of age, and the other at 46. Pokagon died in Cass County, Mich., about 1841.

"Simon Pokagon, a distinguished Pottawattamie Indian, still living near Hartford, Mich., is the only living son of Leopold Pokagon, having been born at Pokagon Village in 1830. He has the distinction of being the best educated and most distinguished full-blooded Indian, probably, in America. He has written much, and delivered many addresses of real literary merit during the past quarter of a century, and when he passes away he will leave no successor in this line worthy of the name. He has managed the band of about 300, of which he has for many years been the acknowledged head, with consummate skill and ability; and although the band, of which he is the most prominent member, has not made much headway in keeping pace with the rapid advance of civilization the past fifty years, yet had it not been for Pokagon,—his education, enlightened views, and influence exerted in the right direction,—it is likely it would have retrograded, disintegrated, and would undoubtedly long since have been scattered to the four winds of heaven. While the old chief has his faults, 'even as you and I,' yet when his history comes to be written in the years to come, he will be accorded the highest round on the ladder of fame among the great men of the once powerful tribe of Pottawattamie Indians."

3. Reverend McCoy, who was a missionary among the Pottawattamies of southern Michigan for several years, has left on record that Pokagon's father was in reality one of those noble red men we read about; that he was talented, and that with his many transactions with the early settlers, was never known to break his word. It is further stated in the record that each year while he was among these Indians, a large body of Sioux passed along the old trail that ran through the Pokagon village, on their way to Maulden, Canada, where they received small annuities from the English government, for fighting against the United States in the war of 1812; and that when this body of Sioux passed through in 1827, they had a boy about ten years old with them, a prisoner they had taken from some other tribe; and that Pokagon, out of pity, bought him for four ponies, saddles and bridles, and adopted him as his own son, taking care of him until of age.

While the old chief lived, no trader dared bring whisky among his people, as he would order it seized and destroyed.

thirty-nine thousand dollars. He afterward visited General Grant while president, with whom he smoked the pipe of peace, receiving thanks for Indian soldiers furnished during the war.

After patiently struggling for years, through opposition and poverty, a portion of the balance due, one hundred and fifty thousand dollars[4] without interest, was finally allowed by the Court of Claims, appealed to the United States Supreme Court, and there affirmed; but was not paid until the fall of 1896.

The old chief was present at the opening of the World's Fair, May 1, 1893. He saw with a critic's eye aliens and strangers from every land take their seats on the great platform in the shadow of the gilded dome of the Administration building; he saw the Duke of Veragua and suite, as well as foreign commissioners, take the platform of honor in front, while he and a few others of his race, the only true Americans, stood in the background, unnoticed and unprovided for. When all was ready, the orchestra struck up the "Columbian March," prayer was offered for all nationalities in a general way, which I suppose of course must have included the Indians. After President Cleveland had responded to the address of welcome by the director, he touched the electric button, and the World's Columbian Exposition was born, filled with life and spirit.

From the time the Columbian Fair was first talked of, the old chief had had a great desire to have the educated people of his race hold a congress there, so as to inform the world of what they had accomplished along the lines of civilization; but he was doomed to be disappointed. On that memorable day he saw all nationalities provided for except the original Americans. It almost broke the old man's heart.

While he stood sadly considering the great wrong to his people, a little girl of his own race, unnoticed before, stepped quietly up to him and, seemingly in pity, handed him some wild flowers. On relating this singular circumstance to a friend on his return home, he added: "I can not fully explain to you why it was, but on receiving the flowers I could not refrain from tears; and even now as I think of it, that same tearful feeling creeps through my soul." It was in such a frame of mind he was inspired to write "The Red Man's Greeting," fitly termed by Professor Swing, of Chicago, "The Red Man's Book of Lamentations." It was

---

4. Notwithstanding Pokagon has labored so many years to procure payment due his people, he has only received an equal share with each member of his band, or, as he states it. "The last child born received the same as I" in consequence of which he has had a hard struggle to gain a livelihood.

published in a booklet made from the manifold bark of the white birch tree. The little unique rustic book has been read with great interest, and highly complimented by the press, both in this country and in Europe, for its wild, rough imagery and native eloquence.[5]

Owing to his disappointment in not securing for his people a congress, he did not take kindly to the World's Fair being held in the city of his father, which is expressed in no doubtful terms in his birch-bark booklet. It was through the spirit breathed out by this little volume that he was solicited by Mayor Harrison and some ladies friendly to his race to attend the Fair as a guest of the city. He finally gave consent and went. On the day following his arrival, a large number of ladies were holding a convention in the parlors of the Palmer House, considering the propriety of giving the educated Indians of the race an opportunity to attend the Fair and hold a congress of their own. They sent a private carriage to the Fair grounds and brought the old chief before them. After explaining to him the object of the meeting, they requested that he would express his feelings in regard to the subject under consideration. He arose amid all the show of dress and the glitter of diamonds, apparently with as much composure as if he was among his own people in his own council-house, and said:—

"I rejoice that you are making an effort, at last, to have the educated people of my race take part in the great celebration. That will be much better for the good of our people, in the hearts of the dominant race, than war-whoops and battle-dances, such as I today witnessed on Midway

---

5. (From the daily *Inter Ocean* during Chicago week of the Fair.)

POKAGON, THE INDIAN POET. APT IN LATIN AND GREEK

Chief Pokagon. chief of the Pottawattamies, is here visiting the Fair. Through his efforts nearly $200,000 have been appropriated by the United States for the Indians through treaties made with his father, Leopold Pokagon, who was the leading chief of the tribe for forty-two years. In 1826, at Tippecanoe, O., one treaty was made, and another at the same place three years later. In 1830 one was made at Chicago, and another in 1833, by which over a million acres of land was ceded to the government. He was present at the Fort Dearborn massacre, Chicago, in 1812. He died in 1840.

Simon Pokagon, the son, has a good education. He is quite a Greek and Latin scholar, and is acknowledged by the government to be the Chief of the Pottawattamies.

On sale at the American Indian village on the Midway is a little booklet with its leaves and cover made of birch bark. Its title is "The Red Man's Greeting." It was written by Simon Pokagon, and is a cry from the Indian heart for the woes of his people. I have reviewed it before in these columns. It is certainly a poem in prose. No one can read it without realizing the "other" side of the Indian question.

Plaisance. It will increase our friends and encourage us. Tomorrow will make the sixtieth year that has passed since my father sold for his tribe over one million acres of land, including the site of this city and the grounds on which the Exposition now stands, for three cents an acre. I have grown old trying to get the pay for my people. I have just returned from the city of the Great Father, where I have been allowed by the Court of Claims one hundred and fifty thousand dollars, which I expect will soon be paid. We wish to rejoice with you, and will accept your invitation with gratitude. The world's people, from what they have so far seen of us on the Midway, will regard us as savages; but they shall yet know that we are human as well as they, and the children of my father will always love those who help us to show that we are *men*."

Perhaps no one person contributed more to swell the vast audience at the Fair on Chicago day than did Pokagon. For two weeks previous, his coming was announced in glowing head-lines by all the leading papers of the city and throughout the United States. He was the great master link between She-gog-ong[6] as an Indian village and Chicago as one of the greatest commercial cities of the world. His father, for forty-two years the leading chief of the Pottawattamies, had owned the city site, including the Exposition grounds. His son Pokagon, the present chief, when a boy, had lived in Chicago; was there when it was transferred to the United States, and had camped many times with his father on the very grounds where stood the "White City." His father, too, had there killed the buffalo and the deer, and over the same ground had many times led his warriors around the head of Lake Michigan. On the morning of Chicago day the opening exercises of the Fair were heralded by sixteen trumpeters sent by General Miles from Fort Sheridan. They were richly attired, resplendent in royal purple and scarlet, decorated and trimmed with lace that glistened like burnished gold in the sunshine. Four of the trumpeters took their position on the Administration building, four on the Columbian arch peristyle, and the others on the Manufactures and Liberal Arts building flanking the lagoon. They first played a fanfare in quartet of "peace on earth and goodwill to men," repeating it all in unison. This was followed by the discharge of cannon as a salute to all nations, which, like heavy thunder,

6. The Algonquin name of Chicago was She-gog-ong, derived from the word "she-gog" (skunk). Locative case: "She-gog-ong ne-de-zhaw"—I am going to Chicago; "She-gog-ong ne-do-je-baw"—I come from Chicago; "She-gog-ong e-zhwan"—Go to Chicago.

rolled through the winding avenues of the White City, dying away in one continuous roar. The trumpeters then played an overture to all the kingdoms of the earth, followed by the "Star-Spangled Banner," with a chorus of two thousand voices, while the vast multitude joined the refrain.

At the west plaza of the Administration building stood the new Liberty Bell awaiting dedication, and rung for the first time on that day by Chief Pokagon. Pushing their way inch by inch through the dense crowd at nine o'clock A.M., appeared Mayor Harrison and the old chief, and others of his tribe, with Miss Sickles, chairman of the Historical Committee, and several maidens of the Cherokee nation, taking their position in front of the new Liberty Bell. The old veteran chief held in his hand a parchment duplicate of the original deed by which, sixty years before, his father conveyed Chicago and the Fair grounds, together with the surrounding country, to the United States. He handed the time-worn treaty deed to Miss Sickles, who, after receiving it, presented it to Mayor Harrison, saying, "With this duplicate I also present you a written request from Chief Pokagon for your consideration. A messenger has also come from the Indian Territory, whose people ask that the mayor will assist in declaring, for the recognition of the world, the advancement made by the Indian in the lines of independence and self-development which have been at the root of our Republic and the magnificence of Chicago; and they ask that he message of the red man may be rung out to the people by the Liberty Bell, a message of peace on earth, good-will toward men, which includes them in the fatherhood of God and in the brotherhood of man."

Receiving the ancient document and the chief's request,[7] the venerable mayor said:—

---

7. The message referred to, as published in the Chicago dailies the morning following Chicago day, was as follows:—

To his honor, the mayor: I have heard with much pleasure that the blood of Pocahontas flows in your veins, and, as one of my people, I call upon you to help the educated Indians of our great country in their efforts to celebrate this great Fair. Many of my people have already come, but have found no place for them in the celebration. The land on which Chicago and the Fair stands, still belongs to my people, as it has never yet been paid for. All we ask from Chicago is that the people help us to come and join with them and the world in telling how great is our common country. We wish to talk for ourselves. The Pottawattamies have a message to deliver to the world, and so have the five civilized tribes of the Indian Territory. We need about two thousand dollars to enable us to hold

"This deed comes from the original possessors,—the only people on earth entitled to it. The Indians had for long ages come to this place, the portage or carrying-place between the great rivers of the West, and the great inland lakes. They pitched their tents upon these shores of blue Michigan, and after their barter was done returned to the Des Plaines River and on to the Mississippi and its twelve thousand miles of tributaries. Chicago has thrived as no city ever before. Twenty-two years ago this city was devastated by a deluge of flame. The story of its suffering went to all quarters of the globe, and the world supposed that, like Niobe, it was in tears, and would continue in tears. But Chicago had *Indian* blood in its veins. I say this as a descendant of the Indians; for I stand here and tell you that Indian blood courses through my veins. I go back to Pocahontas, and Indian blood has wonderfully recuperative powers.[8]

"Chicago sprung phenix-like from its ashes; and this is the evidence,—this White City that has enabled the dreams of poets and the aspirations of architects to be crystallized in white marble and staff, the most beautiful city the world has ever seen.

"It would be considered the product of magic were it not that it exemplifies the audacity of man. Chicago will keep untarnished the site the Indians have given us. Lawlessness will never find—has never found—a foothold here. It may break out at times, but our people love law and order. We should thank the Giver of good for this day. Two

---

our congress in your city, which was once our hunting-grounds. We have given it to you; and now more than one hundred of our race, as educated and progressive as many of our white brothers, would come to make a treaty of peace and progress to last for all time. In making your people rich we have become poor. In the name of the progressive men of my race, who so far have found no place for themselves in the celebration of the year, I ask you and the people of this great city to help us come back and talk with you for one day. We wish to show the world that we are men and brothers, worthy to be called Americans, and fit for citizenship.

SIMON POKAGON.

8. In an article by the chief on "The Future of the Redman" in the August number of the New York *Forum* of 1897, appears the following: "Certain it is that the families of the Harrisons, Rolings, Rogers, and many others tinctured with the Indian blood of Pocahontas, are superior in health to, and fully as strong intellectually and morally, as those families from the same branch of pure white blood. John Randolph of Roanoke, a near descendant of this Indian woman, and strongly marked with our race lines, was several times congressman from Virginia, once United States senator, and minister to Russia. In his times his speeches were more read than any others. His masterly arguments were the pride of his party and the terror of his opponents." The article above referred to has been published in different languages in this country and Europe.

days ago the weather clerk said it would storm today, but Providence has given us a genial sky, and Chicago day is the biggest day ever seen; it will beat Paris's big day.

"I feel confident we shall have over one-half million of people on these grounds to give evidence of their appreciation of the energy, pluck, and audacity which built this fair city."

At the close of the mayor's speech, cheer on cheer arose for Chicago and Mayor Harrison.

After the cheering subsided, Miss Sickles introduced the old chief to the sea of upturned faces. He was dressed in navy blue, but wore upon his head the cap and feathers that indicated his standing in his tribe. With true native dignity the old veteran stepped in front of the bell, and taking hold the rope of red, white, and blue, which had been made especially for the occasion, he paused. There was a look of sadness in his face, showing to a close observer that the weight of years was pressed into a moment of time. Then, realizing the significance of the occasion,—"to link the present with the past,"—he tried to smile to hide his tears as he slowly and sadly tolled the knell of departed time and wrongs forgiven. He ceased, and silence for a time reigned supreme, until broken by "Gloria Halleluiah," which was sung by the vast multitude for the first time on the Fair ground. As the last echoes died away, amid tumultuous cheers, he stepped to the post of honor,— laid aside his tribal cap and feathers. Standing in silence until order was restored, he spoke as follows:—

"Through the untiring effort of a few friends of another race, I greet you! If any of you, my countrymen, feel the sting of neglect because your rights have been ignored in taking part in the world's great Fair until now, I beseech you to lay aside all bitterness of spirit, and with hearts so pure and good that these noble mothers and daughters that so labored in our behalf for this, may rejoice that the kind seed they have sown has not fallen on dry and barren ground.

"Let us not crucify ourselves by going over the bloody trails we have trod in other days, but rather let us look up and rejoice in thankfulness in the present; for out of the storm cloud of darkness that is round about us we now see helping hands stretched out to aid and strengthen us, while above the roar and crash of the cyclone of civilization are heard many voices demanding that to the red man justice *must* be done; demanding that no more agents through party influence shall be appointed to deal with us; demanding that places now filled by Indian agents, incompetent men for the trust, shall be supplied by good and competent men; demanding that no more 'fire water,' the 'beverage of hell,' shall be sold or given to our people at home or abroad; demanding, in words not misunderstood, that we *must* lay aside all tribal relations, and become citizens, kings, and queens of this great Republic!

"The question comes up to us again and again, 'What can be done for the best good of the remnant of our race?' The answer to me is plain and clear, and it matters not how distasteful it may seem to us; we *must* give up the pursuits of our fathers. However dear we love the chase, we MUST give it up. We must teach our children to give up the bow and arrow that is born in their hearts; and, in place of the gun, we must take the plow, and live as white men do. They are all around about our homes. The game is gone never to return; hence it is vain to talk about support from game and fish. Many of our people are now successful in raising grain and stock. What they have done, we all can do. Our children *must* learn that they owe no allegiance to any clan or power on earth except the United States. They must learn to love the Stars and Stripes, and at all times to rejoice that they are American citizens.

"Our children must be educated, and learn the different trades of the white men. Thanks to the Great Spirit, this government has already established a few schools for that purpose; and to learn of the success, you have but to visit the Indian's school on these grounds, examine the work of the children, see the different articles they have made, examine their writing-books, and you will be convinced that they will be able to compete with the dominant race.

"I was pained to learn that some, who should have been interested in our people, discouraged our coming to the Fair, claiming openly that we are heartless, soulless, and godless. Now let us all as one pray the Great Spirit that he will open the eyes of their understanding, and teach them to know that we are human as well as they; teach them to know that,—

> *"Within the recess of the native's soul,*
> *There is a secret place, which God doth hold;*
> *And though the storms of life do war around,*
> *Yet still within, his image fixed is found.*

"I am getting to be an old man. I often feel one foot is uplifted to step into the world beyond. But I am thankful that the measure of my days has been lengthened out, and that I am able to stand before you in this great congress of people, in this four hundredth year of the white man's advent in our fathers' land.

"In my infancy I was taught to love my chief and tribe, but since then the great West has been swallowed up by the white man, and by adoption we are the children of this great Republic; hence we *must* teach loyalty to our children, and solemnly impress upon them that the war-path leads but to the grave. I shall cherish as long as I live the cheering words that have been spoken to me here by ladies, friends of my race. It has strengthened and encouraged me. I have greater faith in the success of the remaining few of my people than ever before. I now realize that the hand of the Great Spirit is open in our behalf; already he has thrown his great search-light upon the vault of heaven, and Christian men and women are reading them in characters of fire well understood, 'The red man is your brother, and God is the Father of all.'"

At the close of the address, amid prolonged cheers, a grand rush was made for the old chief, and both his hands were shaken until his arms gave out.

During the afternoon of that day he was taken to the stock pavilion, where he had been chosen honorary umpire of a game of lacrosse played between the Canadian Iroquois and the Pottawattamies. As he was being conducted to a seat in the press box, he was recognized and cheered by the vast audience that occupied every seat in the great stock amphitheater. During the evening of that day he was the central figure on the magnificent historical float of 1812 drawn by eight beautiful horses. On it was represented, almost true to life, the famous Black Partridge rescuing the white woman, Mrs. Helm, from the savage Pottawattamie's tomahawk during the massacre at Fort Dearborn, while in full blaze of the calcium lights stood the veteran chief, with four Cherokee maidens gaily attired, cheerfully singing their native songs.

The following appeared in the Chicago *Inter Ocean* and other dailies of the city the following day:—

The Son of the Indian Who Once Owned Chicago
Addresses the Multitude

It was entirely in keeping with the spirit of the great day that the central figure of the ceremony should be an Indian, and that Indian a son of the chief who sold to the white people the ground upon which Chicago and the Exposition are located. Incidental to that ceremony was the ringing of the new Liberty Bell on the Administration plaza. Not fewer than ten thousand visitors were crowded about the frame in which the bell wings, when at nine o'clock W. O. McDowell climbed upon a cross-beam, and in a few words explained the significance of the occasion. Miss Emma Sickles, the red man's friend, introduced Chief Pokagon, who was dressed in army blue, but wore upon his head the cap and feathers that indicated his standing in his tribe.

After Miss Sickles had spoken of the contract which gave to the civilized world the location of Chicago, Pokagon seized the rope and swung the ponderous bell until the entire Exposition grounds rang with its notes. Then he stepped to the post of honor, laid aside his cap and feathers, and began his address.

Pokagon is a man of such majestic proportions and mien that he would attract attention in any company. His face, of course, is of a deep bronze, and his features are regular and clear cut.

Few men have a better command of language. He spoke of the relation of the Indians to the white people, and hoped for universal peace for the future. At the conclusion of his speech he held an informal reception, shaking by the hand probably one thousand persons.

The old chief had scarcely returned to his home in Michigan, after taking part in the celebration on Chicago day, when he was again sent for by Mayor Harrison to return and assist in taking part in the closing ceremonies of the great Columbian Fair; but when he arrived in the city, and inquired for the mayor, he was astonished to learn that he had been cruelly murdered at his home the previous night. This so saddened the heart of the old chief that the closing ceremonies were to him more like a funeral than a day of rejoicing. I herewith subjoin an article clipped from the Chicago *Tribune*, published the following day:—

Indians Loved the Genial Mayor

How he befriended Pokagon and promised to help his race

It is said Carter Harrison never forgets to fulfil a promise. Chicago day he received from Miss Emma C. Sickles the deed to the city sent him by Chief Pokagon. He then and there promised to help the chief gain recognition at the Fair, and also the money which the government still owed the Pottawattamie band for the ground on which the White City stands. The last kind act of the dead mayor's life was to write to Pokagon, inclosing the necessary money for his expenses, and a cordial invitation for the chief to become his guest and take part in the closing ceremonies of the great Fair.

It was through Miss Sickles's efforts that Pokagon was brought here on Chicago day; and as the two assisted the mayor on the greatest day of the Fair, they again were to take part together in the closing ceremonies, when at midnight the great Columbian bell was to toll its protest against the destruction of the White City, and call for a resurrection next summer, when the progressive Indians who have sought so long for recognition would take part.

The bell was tolled, but at sunset, when for the last time its solemn tones resounded among the massive columns and through the great halls of the White City, in memory of him who was to have been the central figure of the great occasion, the aged Pokagon stood with head uncovered, too unnerved by the great sorrow which had come upon him to assist in the tolling. But after the Daughters of the American Revolution had struck the sixty-eight taps that numbered out the years of the dead man's life, the gray-haired Pottawattamie feebly mounted the platform at the base of the bell, and, with tears in the furrows of his cheeks, spoke a few words in remembrance of the friend whose guest he was.

Said they were Brothers

"He said we were brothers," began Pokagon, in a voice scarce above a whisper, "and I loved him as such, for in his veins ran the blood of my race—Pocahontas. On Chicago day we both stood beside this bell. He then promised that he would help my people. I knew he would keep his word, and two days ago I received an invitation to become his guest. Gladly I came, but while still on the way I learned that he was dead. In my sorrow I knew not what to do. He alone at the Fair has welcomed those of my race who have climbed the heights of manhood. He was to help my people get the money promised them for the land on which stands the city he helped to make great. On the natal day of his city, he bade the Pottawattamies and all progressive Indians welcome. Today we mourn him, for every Indian has lost a friend." Here the chief broke down, and Chairman W. O. McDowell told a story of a little boy seven years of age, who wrote to him asking it it was true that the land on which the Fair stands was bought from the Indians for three cents an acre and never paid for. He wanted the bell taken away until it was paid for, as he did not want liberty to ring out from land which was not paid for.

John W. Hutchinson sang the Indian hunting song; and the last official words about the Columbian bell, so far as the Fair is concerned, were spoken by Miss Sickles in a brief but stirring address in memory of Carter Harrison, the friend of the Indians. She said:—

"Pokagon has told you how firm a friend he had found in your dead magistrate, but he has not told you of the difficulties he had to overcome before he could gain recognition for himself or his people at this great Exposition, and how at last the hand outstretched to help him was that of your mayor.

Mayor Harrison Helped Him

"Pokagon has stood at the door of the congress of religions, but there was no place for him or his people on the program. He has asked for recognition for his people here, but not until Mayor Harrison outstretched the hand of welcome could he find it.

"The time has come when the Indian is no longer a savage; he is a man, and demands recognition as such; he will never be satisfied with less. He wishes to be an American among Americans, and this is the message he sends you."

These were the last words spoken from the bell. Its mission is over so far as the Fair is concerned, and there could be no more fitting conclusion than a request from the aborigines of this great country for equal liberty with those who have succeeded him.

Pokagon Remembered

At the close of the Columbian Fair, Chief Pokagon received of Luella D. Smith, the poetess, of Hudson, N. Y., a volume of her poems, "Wind Flowers," in exchange for the "Red Man's Greeting." On receipt of the book he said, "I trust you will not fail to leave something in verse for the benefit of our race." On his return home he received from the lady the following poem dedicated to his people:—

The Cry of Cain

My punishment I can not bear:
I keep for ay the heart of care:
Forever hearing from the ground
The cries of blood from out the wound
Of Abel, my brother.

His was this broad and grand domain;
The hills and vales, the sweep of plain,
The hunting grounds, the rivers wide,—
They all belonged, before he died,
To Abel, my brother.

But he is dead. I hear it call—
The blood my blow of wrath let fall.
I wear for ay the murderer's brand,
For I have killed him with my hand,—
Killed Abel, my brother.

The rivers murmur words he gave:
The mountains all the echoes save;
The woods hold music of his voice:
Their names were given by the choice
Of Abel, my brother.

I drove him from his fair estate
From East to West, with endless hate;
At last he lay beneath my tread,

Brave son of forests, stark and dead,
Red Abel, my brother.

"My brother's keeper!" No, not I.
I will not heed my brother's cry.
Silence should come at least with death.
Why speaks he still, who is but breath?
Dead Abel, my brother.

Have I not builded high and well?
Does not the world my glory tell?
Among the nations I am great.
"How came I to this vast estate?"
O Abel, my brother'

My cities stand on dead men's bones:
I hear the sobs; I feel the groans.
I know the grief none may express,—
The hate, the woe, the bitterness
For Abel, my brother.

The ground beneath me cries, "Redress!"
The skies above me shout, "Confess!"
His blood is rising from the sod,
And speaking in the ears of God
For Abel, my brother.

No nation dares to do me harm;
The brand that saves me from alarm
Before mankind, affrights of God.
I wander in dark "Lands of Nod"
For Abel, my brother.

Afar from Eden's groves I roam,—
Afar from rest, afar from home,
The "Sons of God" my soul disdain;
I am, alas! the murderer (Cain)
Of Abel, my brother.

Have I not made my steeples tall,
Devoted to the Lord of all?
O, land beneath that ever quakes!
O, heart of pain that ever aches
For Abel, my brother!

Afar from God, afar from life,
I hold my place by power and strife;
And oft my children's blood is shed
Because of him I conquered,—
Brave Abel, my brother!

What then! The children of his race,
With slightest hold on power and place,
Bemoan, alas, their cruel fate;
The weak crushed ever by the great.
Poor Abel, my brother!

They hold to me their wounded hands;
With pride they claim their ancient lands.
Downtrodden, yet they still arise,
And call the vengeance of the skies
For Abel, my brother.

I can not tear my cities down;
I can not God's vast voices drown.
This curse is more than I can bear;
I turn to penitence and prayer.
O Abel, my brother!

The past can never be undone.
The new day brings the rising sun
To light the way of duty now
To children with the dusky brow
Of Abel, my brother.

The while I follow ancient wrong,
Though God withhold his judgment long,

I bear through all his universe,
The lasting burden of his curse.
O Abel, my brother!

Would I were free to choose aright
Before this day is lost in night!
O God, forgive my selfish sin
And help me yet thy love to win
With Abel, my brother!

It is estimated that during his lifetime Pokagon has interpreted into his mother tongue at least a thousand sermons as they were delivered; he was also organist at all church services during the same period. All Indians who have ever heard him speak in their native language, declare him to be a great orator.

During the past five years the chief has addressed many pioneer meetings, always attracting large crowds. He has furnished many contributions to such leading magazines as the *Arena, Forum, Chautauquan, Harper's Magazine, Review of Reviews*, and many others, which have been highly complimented both in this country and in Europe. He has been called by the press, "the red-skin bard," the "Longfellow of his race," and the "grand old man."

True to his Indian nature, the old chief never exhibits vanity, or appears in any wise puffed up or boastful over any honors conferred upon him; neither does he refer to them unless interrogated, when, like an unbiased witness in court, he simply answers the questions asked him.

BY THE PUBLISHERS

The Algonquin Language

BY THE AUTHOR

I n presenting "Queen of the Woods" to the public, I realize that many of its readers will inquire why so many Indian words are used. All such will please bear in mind that the manuscript was first written in the Algonquin language, the only language spoken by me until fourteen years of age, and that in translating it into English, many parts of it seem to lose their force and euphony, insomuch that I deeply regret that "Queen of the Woods" can not be read by the white people in my own language. It is indeed mortifying for me to consider that outside of the proper names of lakes, streams, and places, our language is being almost entirely ignored by the incoming race, while other languages of foreign birth are entering largely into the English dialect; and our children, who are being educated in the white man's schools, are forsaking and forgetting their mother tongue.

In consideration of the fact that the language of the great Algonquin family, which once was spoken by hundreds of thousands throughout more than half of North America, is fast passing away, I have retained such Indian words and expressions as appear in "Queen of the Woods," as monuments along the way, to remind the reader in after-generations, that such a language as ours was once spoken throughout this loved land of my fathers.

I also wish to leave on record the fact that our language is not a sort of "gibberish," as some believe, containing a few hundred words, but that, on the contrary, it contains at least twenty thousand words, aside from their many variations.

There are only seventeen letters in the pure Algaic language: four vowels, *a, e, i, o,* and thirteen consonants, *b, c, d, g, h, j, k, m, n, p, s, t, w.* They pronounce *f* and *v* like *b* or *p;* and *l* and *r* like *n.* Like every other language, it has its own orthography.

The sound of the vowels never changes. The four vowels are pronounced as follows: *a,* as in father (as änäkänän, mats); *e,* as in met (as ĕtĕg, what there is; ĕtä, only); *i,* as in pin (as ĭnĭnĭ, a man; ĭwĭdĭ, there); *o,* as in note (as in ŏdŏn, his mouth; ŏkŏge, its bill). These rules have no exception in our language. Where two or more vowels come together, each one must be sounded.

There are some diphthongs in this language; for instance, *ai, ei, oi, ia, ie, io,* and both vowels must be distinctly sounded. Examples: Mĭsäï (fish), pronounced mĭ-säï; äpäkwei (a mat to cover a lodge), pronounced ä-pä-kwĕï; säiägiäd (whom thou lovest), pronounced sä-ĭä-gĭ-äd.

There are nine parts of speech in our language, as follows:—

1. The Substantive; as, inini (man), ikwe (woman), wigiwam (a lodge).
2. The Pronoun; as, nin (I), kin (thou), win (he, she, or it).
3. The Verb; as, nin gigit (I speak), ki nōndäm (thou hearest).
4. The Adjective; as, gwänätch (beautiful), matchi (bad).
5. The Number; as, midässwĭ (ten), nigtänä (twenty).
6. The Preposition; as, näwäii (in the midst).
7. The Adverb; as, sĕsikä (suddenly), nibiwä (much).
8. The Conjunction; as, gaie (and), kishpin, (if).
9. The Interjection; as, hōi! (hallo!); häw! (go on!).

I believe that in our language there is greater liberty in the transposition of the words in a sentence than in any other, unless it may be the Latin language; and even in that the changes can not be made without suffering greater violence than in ours. For example, we will take the following sentence: "K'oss" (thy father) "ta-bi-ija" (will come) "oma" (here) "nongom" (today).

Example

K'oss ta-bi-ija oma nongom: Thy father will come here today.
Nongom oma ta-bi-ija k'oss: Today here will come thy father.
Ta-bi-ija k'oss oma nongom: Will come thy father here today.
Nongom oma k'oss ta-bi-ija: Today here thy father will come.
Oma nongom k'oss ta-bi-ija: Here today thy father will come.
Ta-bi-ija k'oss nongom oma: Will come thy father today here.
K'oss nongom ta-bi-ija oma: Thy father today will come here.
Oma ta-bi-ija nongom k'oss: Here will come today thy father.

Another peculiarity of our language is that in some cases men have their own interjections, and the women have theirs; for instance, the men and boys will say, "Ataw-a!" or "ti-we!" and the women and girls will say, "Nia!" or "nego!"—all meaning oh! or alas! The difference is so sharp, that it would be a ridiculous blunder for an astonished man to say "Nia!" or for a surprised woman to say "Ataw-a!"

There are in our language many particles, or little words, some of which precede and others follow verbs; for example, "na," one of question, and "sa," one of answer. Take the sentence, "Ki sägiä nä Kiji-Mänitō? (Dost thou love God?)"—"Nin sagia sa (I love him)."

Another particle is "da," of condition: "Nin da-ija kishpin (I would go if, etc.)."

The particles "wi" or "wa," of will or intention: "Nin wi-niba (I will go to sleep);" "Nin wi-onishka (I will get up)."

There is in our language scarcely a preposition that precedes the substantive, but they are generally connected with it, forming a single word, and must be conjugated with the verb.

We have no "articles" in our language; some have supposed "aw" in "aw-ikwe" to be an article, but it does not denote *the* woman, but this or that woman.

We have no separate pronoun for gender, "win" signifying he, she, or it; but we use different words for the individuals of different sex by prefixing the word "nabe" to the masculine gender, and "ikwe" to those of female gender; as, "Nabe-suc-see" (buck or male deer), "Ikwe-suc-see" (a doe or female deer). In English, when several persons are referred to of like gender, many times it is extremely difficult to understand, by the pronoun, which one is referred to, but in our language that doubt never occurs.

Another peculiarity in our language is the shortening of words in forming phrases; for example, "onindgima" (hand), "ni-nindg" (my hand), "ki-nindg" (thy hand), "onindg" (his hand).

Again, take "oossima" (father), "noss" (my father), "k'oss" (thy father), "ossan" (his father); "wegimind" (mother), "ninga" (my mother), "kiga" (thy mother), "ogin" (his mother).

Relationship in our language is much more clearly defined than in the English. Take, for example, "my uncle:" We would say "nimishome," which signifies "my father's brother," and "nijishe," which means "my mother's brother." "My aunt" is expressed by "ninsigos" (my father's sister), and "ninoshe" (my mother's sister), and so on through the different lines of relationship, which generally are expressed and defined by a single word.

In concluding this brief sketch of the Algaic dialect, I wish to state that all parts of speech hinge on the verb, and nearly all the words in our language can be transformed into verbs. The learned, who have studied our language well, and have become familiar with its construction, declare that it is a wonderful dialect; that it is perfect in its own way, and has many beauties not to be found in modern languages. The verb in the Algonquin idiom is indeed the supreme chief of all other parts of speech. It has been compared by a learned philologist to Atlas carrying the world on his shoulders. If such a comparison is allowable, I will venture a more modern one, and say it is more like the sun that holds in his embrace all the bodies of the solar system, drawing into its magical circle all other parts of speech, causing them to breathe, move, suffer, or rejoice in such manner and in such situations as is most pleasing to it.

Names of the Twelve Months

Manito-gisiss—The moon of the spirit. (January.)
Namebini-gisiss—The moon of suckers—fish. (February.)
Onabini-gisiss—The moon of crust on the snow. (March.)
Bebokwedagiming-gisiss—The moon of breaking of snow-shoes. (April.)
Wabigon-gisiss—The moon of flowers and bloom. (May.)
Odeimini gisiss—The moon of strawberries—heart-berries. (June.)
Miskwimini-gisiss—The moon of raspberries—red berries. (July.)
Min-gisiss—The moon of whortleberries. (August.)
Manominike-gisiss—The moon of gathering the wild rice. (September.)
Binakwi-gisiss—The moon of falling leaves. (October.)
Gashkadino-gisiss—The moon of freezing. (November.)
Manito-gisissons—The little moon of the spirit. (December.)

The word "gisiss" means both sun and moon; the moon we call tibiki-gisiss (the night sun), "tibik" (night).

"Gijig," or "gijigad" (day); "Nigogwan" (two days), etc.

In speaking of the time, we say such a moon is so many days old; for instance, Manito-gisis (January) "Nongom" (today) nijgwanagisi is the second day of January; and so on through all the different days of each moon during the year.

In speaking of the time of day we place the numeral representing the hour before the word, "dibaigan," meaning "o'clock;" for instance, Bejig dibaigan—one o'clock; nig dibaigan—two o'clock; niswi dibaigan—three o'clock; and so on.

The following numerals, with slight variations, were once used by all the tribes of the great Algonquin family:—

Bejig—One.
Nij—Two.
Niswi—Three.
Niwin—Four.
Nanan—Five.
Ningotwaswi—Six.
Nijwaswi—Seven.
Nishwaswi—Eight.
Jangaswi—Nine.
Midaswi—Ten.
Midaswi ashi bejig—Eleven.
Midaswi ashi nig—Twelve.
Midaswi ashi niswi—Thirteen.
Midaswi ashi niwin—Fourteen.
Midaswi ashi nanan—Fifteen.
Midaswi ashi ningotwaswi—Sixteen.
Midaswi ashi nijwasi—Seventeen.
Midaswi ashi nishwaswi—Eighteen.
Midaswi ashi Jangaswi—Nineteen.
Nigtana—Twenty.
Nigtana ashi bejig—Twenty-one.
Nigtana ashi nij—Twenty-two.
Nigtana ashi niswi—Twenty-three.
Nisimidana—Thirty.
Nisimidana ashi bejig—Thirty-one.
Nimidana—Forty.
Nanimidana—Fifty.
Ningottwasimidana—Sixty.
Nijwasimidana—Seventy.
Nishwasimidana—Eighty.
Jangasimidana—Ninety.
Ningotwak—One hundred.
Ningotwak ashi bejig—One hundred and one.
Ningotwak ashi Nij—One hundred and two.

Ningotwak ashi midaswi—One hundred and ten.

Ningotwak ashi midaswi ashi bejig—One hundred and eleven.

Ningotwak ashi midaswi ashi ningotwaswi—One hundred and sixteen.

Ningotwak ashi nigtana—One hundred and twenty.

Ningotwak ashi nigtana ashi nanan—One hundred and twenty-five.

Nijwak—Two hundred.

Nijwak ashi nanimidana ashi nanan—Two hundred and fifty-two.

Niswak—Three hundred.

Niwak—Four hundred.

Nanwak—Five hundred.

Ningotwaswak—Six hundred.

Nijwaswak—Seven hundred.

Nishwaswak—Eight hundred.

Jangaswak—Nine hundred.

Midaswak—One thousand, etc., etc.

The reader of the foregoing table will please bear in mind that the conjunction, "ashi," rendered in English, means "and," but it is only used in our language to join numerals; hence when we say, "midaswi ashi bejig," it is equivalent to saying in English, "Ten and one are eleven," and so on up to twenty; and from twenty up to one hundred, and so on, as exemplified in the foregoing table.

Wherever the word "ashi" appears in our language, it always means that the numbers it connects are to be added together. In common usage, between "ten" and "twenty" we omit "nigtana" (twenty), and simply place "ashi" before one of the digits, "ten" of course being understood; for instance, "ashi bejig, 11," "ashi nij, 12," "ashi niswi, 13," and so on. You will further observe from the table that by adding "dana" in certain form to the digits we express 30, 40, 50, 60, 70, 80, etc., and by adding "wak" to the digits we express 100, 200, 300, 400, etc.

Multiplying Numbers

Abiding—once.

Nijing—twice.

Nissing—three times.

Niwig—four times.

Naning—five times.
And so on.

Examples

Nijing ki ga-dipak onigonan Kije-Manito: God will judge us twice.

Kitchitwa Paul naning gi-bashanjeowa auami ewin ondgi: Saint Paul was flogged five times for religion's sake.

Peter nongom tibikad nissing ki gad-agonwetam: Peter, this night thou shalt deny me three times.

Ordinal Numbers

Netam—the first, or firstly.
Eko-nijing—the second, or secondly.
Eko-nising—the third, or thirdly.
Eko-niwing—the fourth, or fourthly.
Eko-nananing—the fifth, or fifthly.
Eko-ningotwatching—the sixth, or sixthly.
And so on.

Example

Kitchi ganasongewin eko-niwing Kige-Manito o ganasongewinan: The fourth command of God is a great commandment.

Cardinal Numbers Transformed Into Verbs

Bejig, one,	Nin bejig,	I am alone.
	Ki begig,	thou art one.
	o begig,	he or she is one.
Nig, two,	nin nijimin,	We are two.
	Ki nigim,	you are two.
	nigiwag,	they are two.

And so on indefinitely. All numeral verbs, animate or inanimate, may be conjugated in all the tenses and moods.

Having presented a very few of the peculiarities of our dialect, I trust you will bear in mind, as you consider them, that they are but a few objects scattered along the shore, while the great ocean lies unexplored beyond; yet, having studied them, you will be better able to form a more correct conception of the beauty, perfection, and magnitude of our language, than you otherwise could have done.

It has been said that Greek is the language of the gods, that Latin is the language of heroes, and that French is the language of lovers and novelists; and Pokagon might consistently add that the Algaic language is the three in one, symmetrically interwoven in nature's great loom.

> *"Let foreign nations of their language boast,*
> *And, proud, with skilful pen, man's fate record;*
> *I like the tongue which speak our men, our coast;*
> *Who can not dress it well want wit, not word."*

I

O n my return home from Twinsburg, O., where I had attended the
white man's school for several years, I had an innate desire to retire
into the wild woods, far from the haunts of civilization, and there enjoy
myself with bow and arrow, hook and line, as I had done before going to
school. Judging from my returning love of the chase, and from various
conversations with educated people of the white race, I have come to
the conclusion that there is a charm about hunting and fishing, planted
deep in the human heart by Nature's own hand, that requires but little
cultivation to lead the best educated of even the most civilized races to
engage heartily in the sport. Hence I have been forced to the conclusion
that when our children are educated, and return from school to live
among their own people, unless places can be secured for them away
from the influences that cluster about them, the result of their education
must necessarily in some cases prove disappointing to those who have
labored so ardently in their behalf. In fact I have personal knowledge of
a few cases where educated children of our race, instead of influencing
their own people to a higher standard of civilization, have themselves
fallen back into the ancient customs of their own people. This, however,
should in nowise discourage our educators, or be regarded by them as
an impeachment of the possibilities of our children; for I believe with
all my heart that if white children were placed under like conditions and
circumstances, the result would be similar.

I knew no other language but my mother tongue until past twelve
years of age. In those days I took great pleasure in hunting, fishing,
and trapping with an old man by the name of Bertrand. There are
many white men yet living who were personally acquainted with that
remarkable man. He was a person well calculated to please and instruct
a boy in his knowledge of the habits of animals, and of places and things
with which he was personally acquainted. He was of medium height,
uncommonly broad shouldered, and well developed in body and limb.
When laughing, or excited in talking, he opened his mouth so wide
that his great double teeth could be plainly seen. He always appeared
in the best of spirits, having the most hearty laugh of any man I ever
knew. As old as I now am, I would walk twenty miles to hear such a
laugh. His skin was dark for an Indian, notwithstanding he claimed to
be one-quarter French. When speaking of himself, he always talked as

if he was a white man. On public occasions among our people, owing to his strength and courage, he was regarded as a sort of police force. I recollect one day during a feast some "au-qua" (women) came running to him in great excitement, telling him some half-breeds had brought "awsh-kon-tay-ne-besh" (firewater) with them, and were giving some to little boys. He started for them on the double-quick, and before they realized what he was doing, he seized all their bottles and broke them against a rock. There were three in the party, and they all rushed for him with sticks and clubs. He knocked each one down in turn with a single blow of his fist. As they lay on the ground, a white man present said, "Bertrand, you struck those Indians awful blows." The old man straightened himself up, saying, "Ae (Yes) me tells you me did. Au-nish-naw-be-og (Indians) hab no idea how hard a white man can strike." For that timely reproof he was given a place at the head of the feast.

He prided himself in speaking English, which he always tried to do if any were present who he thought understood the language.

Among his white neighbors, he was always referred to as "the 'Injun' who murders the English language." A short time after my return from school I called on the old man. I told him that I had just returned from three years' hard study, and would like to have him take mother and me to some wild retreat where I might spend my vacation in hunting and fishing. He seemed highly pleased with the idea, and told me that he knew of a place up big "Sebe" that could be reached by boat in less than one day's sail, where there was an old abandoned wigwam. It was the wildest place that could be found within fifty miles, and there was an abundance of game and fish. Arrangements were made at once, whereby mother and I were to bring our goods to the river on the following day, where he would meet us with his big dugout canoe. As agreed, we all met on the banks of the beautiful "Sebe," loaded our goods into the boat, and pushed off from shore, he at the paddle and I at the helm, with mother and Maw-kaw, our family dog, as passengers. About noon, as we were quietly making our way up the stream, we caught sight of "mi-tchi-sib-wan" (an osprey) with folded wings plunging headlong with the roar of a rocket into the water a short distance from "o-tchi-man" (our boat), and while yet the water surged and foamed where she went down, she arose to the surface, and tried to rise in air, but could not, floundering about in a zigzag course toward the shore. We gave chase with the boat, and as we overhauled the struggling bird we saw, to our surprise, that she had clutched her claws into the back and near the head of "ogaw" (a pickerel) so large that she could not raise it above the surface of the water, and was trying in vain to loose her hold. The old man seized his dipnet, scooped up both osprey and fish, and dropped them into the bottom of the boat. He then grasped with all his might into the gills of the fish, while I seized the osprey with both hands about the wings. We then pulled the unhappy pair apart,—while the old dog continued to whine as if a tom-tom was being beaten in his ears. "Vell, vell," exclaimed the old man, "I kakkalate dat me by dis chase, and the funny catch, do make you feel gooder than to be at school good many years." He then dropped the fish into the bottom of the boat and asked, "Sime, what one of these two do you feel badest for and villing to let go,—dat bud or de vish?" I replied, "The bird, of course." He then asked "nin-gaw" (my mother) the same question, who replied likewise. He then said, "Dat be right; it's not in uman natre to veel bad for vishes, so we will keep de vish, and eat 'im tonight, and let de bud go." I then asked, "Can you explain why we feel more sorrow for bin-es-si (the bird), when in fact she got fast in trying to kill the innocent gi-go (fish)?"

He replied, "I tink me by I can. You know, Sime, dat de vish hab no love at all; da eat um up one an uder,—eat um their own shilren,—and we like to eat um vish, but no like um osprey." He then grasped hold of the bird's tail-feathers and pulled them out, saying, "Now let 'im go; des quills am good for your cap like um mi-gi-si mig-wan (eagle quills)." The old man now became much excited, and as we rode along, he would point to where he had trapped "jang-we-she" (mink), "wa-jask" (muskrat), and "a-se-pan" (coon). At times he would laugh out most heartily in telling how some animals had outwitted him, springing and upsetting his traps; then in telling how he had finally succeeded in catching them, would again laugh more heartily than before.

Just as "gi-siss" (the sun) was going down, we reached our landing-place. The shore on either side was fringed with rushes, flags, and golden-rod, and grasses tall between; and scattered here and there wild roses breathed their rich perfume, scenting the evening air.

Leaving "tchi-man" (the boat), we ascended the banks of the stream, and went some distance round an abrupt headland, beyond which lay "o-ga-be-shi-win aki" (our camping ground). It was indeed a strange, romantic place. A great wigwam there stood. Apparently it had been located so as not to be seen by any that might pass up and down "se-bin" (the stream). It was built of logs of giant size, and, one might well conclude, was intended for wigwam and "wa-ka-i'-gan" (fort) as well. The grounds about were carpeted with "mash-kos-su" (grass). The underbrush had been cleared off years before, leaving the towering trees, which hung their archways of green high above the lawn. As we opened the door of the deserted wigwam, it creaked on its hinges like the cry of murder, which "pas-we-we" (echo) repeated in one continuous wailing through "mit-ig" (the woods). Old dog Maw-kaw, startled at the sound, bellowed out a howl-like cry, which, intermixed with the shrieking roar, died away, leaving a strange impress on the soul! Slowly we entered in. Birds flew all about the spacious room, chirping a wild alarm, and brushing our heads with their wings to frighten us away. "O-was-is-swan" (their nests) hung from roof and wall throughout the room. Soon they quieted down, taking to their nests again, but watched us with suspicious eyes. In one corner of the room, was "mi-chi bo-daw-wan" (a huge fireplace), with chimney built of "mit-i-gons" (sticks) and "wa-bi-gan" (clay); in it, we built a hasty "ish-ko'-te" (fire).

Unlike most men of our race, the old man would dress "gi-go" (the fish) and cook it, too. This, with "maw-da-min" (corn cakes) and salt, furnished a splendid meal, of which we ate, thanking the Great Spirit, the cook, and the bird that caught the fish. As night came on, with our blankets wrapped about us, we all lay down to sleep. By the embers' red light, bats were seen flitting about the spacious room, dodging here and there, and then out of sight, while, with a soft, whizzing sound, "ja-gash-an-dawe" (flying squirrels) passed and repassed above us in curved lines from wall to wall.

It was indeed an ancient, novel place. Long before the break of day, "ak-i-we-si" (the old man) rose and started homeward, as he had promised his family he would be home at noon. I seized my bow and arrows, telling mother I might not be in until after sunrise. "Go on," she said, "only leave Maw-kaw with me." After seeing the old man safely off "pin-dig-ki tchi-man" (in his boat), I carefully climbed to the top of the high headland we had passed around the night before, which like a sentinel, for untold centuries, had guarded the river's valley deep below. I there found an open field, which, from all appearance, had been used during the Indian wars as a lookout for enemies. Here by the faint light of the moon and the glimmering of the stars I dimly surveyed the wild region about me.

It was a beautiful, quiet morning. All nature slept, until the morning feathered bells rang out—"Whip-poor-will! Whip-poor-will!

Whip poor-will!" Slowly, but surely, the curtain of night was lifted from the stage of the woodland theater; above me, one by one the stars hid themselves, the moon grew pale; while all the warblers of the woods opened their matinée, free to all, chanting from unnumbered throats, "Rejoice and praise Him! Rejoice and be glad! Rejoice! Rejoice!" Just as the sun tinged the topmost branches of the highland trees, a white fog-cloud appeared above the winding river as far as eye could reach. It looked as though the stream had risen from its ancient bed, and was floating in mid-air. As in wonder and admiration I gazed upon it, a gentle breeze bore it away far beyond the valley from which it arose; and yet it still retained all the curves and angles of the stream until it passed beyond my sight.

While enraptured, there I stood, beholding the beautiful scenery hung by Nature's hand, and listening to the woodland choir, loud the alarm birds (blue jays) screamed out their hawk-like cries. Abruptly the concert closed, and and all was still! Looking up, I saw advancing toward me across the open field, a herd of deer, feeding as they came. Quietly stepping behind a bush, I selected the patriarch of the flock, and as he passed broadside before me, in three heart-beats of time, I three successive arrows sent into his side. He ran one breath, and headlong, dying fell. Quickly bleeding and disemboweling him, I carried him across my shoulders down a trail through the woods toward the old wigwam. Coming to "mit-ig" (a fallen tree) of monstrous size, I laid the deer thereon; and while resting there, I heard the sweet voice of my mother, singing in her native tongue,—

> "From Greenland's icy mountains,
> From India's coral strand,
> Where Afric's sunny fountains,
> Roll down their golden sand,
> From many an ancient river,
> From many a palmy plain,
> They call us to deliver
> Their land from error's chain."

I had heard her sing it many times before, but never did it reach my soul so touchingly as then. Stooping low so as to get a view below the branches of the trees, I could plainly see the old log cabin, and my mother in front of it. I listened until she sang the whole of that beautiful hymn. It so filled my heart with love divine that in my soul I saw Jesus standing with one hand on the sinner's head and the other resting on the throne of the Great Spirit, saying, "Come unto me." After singing each stanza, and sometimes when half finished she would pause and listen, as if she loved to hear the echoing angel of the woods join in the refrain. As she closed the sacred song, I approached cautiously behind her, and threw my burden down. She screamed aloud, and turning quickly around, gazed a moment in silence, then laughed until all the woods replied. She took hold of the arrows, still fast in his side; praised me for my unforgotten skill; would feel his newly grown, soft, and velvet horns, exclaiming, "Kwaw-notch, kwaw-notch maw-mawsh-kay-she (beautiful, beautiful deer)! How could you have o-daw (the heart) to take nin bim-a'-dis-win (his life)?" After breakfast she skinned the deer, and prepared the meat for jerked venison for future use, according to our ancient custom.

While living in that secluded place, I felt a freedom and independence unknown to civilization. There, undisturbed, I could hunt and fish, contemplating the romantic beauties and wonderful grandeur of the forests about me. While in communion with the Great Spirit, I could feel, as my fathers had before me, that I was chief of all I surveyed.

II

Near the summer's close, while living there, a little maiden, ever now and then, appeared across the stream, with waist of red and skirt of brown, with raven tresses floating in the breeze, following up, but never down the stream. She was always singing, as she gaily tripped along, in mimicry of the music of the birds. Sometimes in her songs, in fancy I could hear and see close by, in bush or brake, the bobolink tuning his voice to cheer his nesting mate. At other times I would look up, *almost* convinced that I could see him dancing in the air, on wing, rising and falling with time and tune, then at the close alighting on the bush from whence he rose. Then, changing time and tune, in fancy I could see some robin perched on top most bough of tree above, pouring forth his song in tones of richest melody. At times, a snow-white deer about the maiden played in circles, like the lamb; and again, after she had passed along and out of sight, like a dog hunting for his master, he would follow on her track. At first I felt impressed that she must be from the happy hunting-ground beyond; and how it was that she could mimic woodland birds, and throw her voice across the stream, and so deceive my ears, was to me a hidden mystery.

While I was fishing along the river's bank for several-days, each morning she so appeared while I was all alone, awakening such sacred feelings in my soul that I held it as a vital secret from my mother.

One morning just before the rising sun, I stood upon the river's shore watching the maid in admiration of her warbling song, when a gentle footstep reached my ears, and looking up, there stood "nin-gaw" (my mother) close beside me. Quietly she said, "Ne-gwis-esh (my son), why are you here at such an early hour as this?" Hiding the real feelings of my heart, I pointed out to her the maid beyond the stream, and said, "Do hear her sing; and see that deer of white around her play." She replied, "Ne-gwis-esh (my son), ne-wob-quay-zans (I see the girl), but hear no song except the songs of pe-nay-shen-wog (birds)." I then said, "O-gaw-shi-maw (mother), she has the time, tune, and song of all the feathered warblers of the woods. Come, sit down upon this log, and listen." She complied with my request, and as she harkened most intently, gazing in all directions, finally said, "Gwai-ak (surely), it must be nin bi-ba-giwin (her voice)

I hear, and in nin-ga-mon (her song) she brings before me me-no-ma (the bobolink), ope-tchi (the robin), and kiki-bïko-meshi (lark); and what seems so strange and droll to me is, it really sounds as if they were on this side of se-bin (the river), near by us; but when I look for them, none can be seen. It must be she is from Man-i-to Au-ke (the spirit world) beyond." During the remainder of that day, my anxiety greatly increased to learn all I could about the woodland maid and the deer of white, and so I concluded to cross the stream, as soon as I could construct a boat for that purpose.

On the following day I went to work with a will, made a small bark canoe large enough to carry one, and launched it at close of day in a bay close by. The next morning before the break of day, I dressed myself with moccasins and pants, all of deerskin made, wearing a birch-bark cap with quills and feathers trimmed. Thus attired in native style, with bow and arrows armed, I went forth, and in my new-made "tchi-man," crossed the river deep and broad. As I neared the other shore, all was still. No breeze disturbed the glass-like surface of the stream; every leaf was motionless, and quiet as the morning air. No artist hand could paint the beauty of the inverted shore as in the water it appeared, fringed with trees, brush, grass, flags, and flowers, with sky below deep down as heaven is high. Carefully I rowed my frail bark under some overhanging willow brush that fringed the shore, and there, almost concealed, with deep anxiety watched and listened, that I might catch with eye or ear the little maiden's first approach. Nor waited long, for soon I heard the bobolink, dancing on the wing, rising and falling with its tune of flute-like notes that seldom fail to reach the lover's heart. It ceased, and then the robin poured forth its thrilling roundelay of love just above me. Hark! I faintly hear some muffled footsteps near, and peering through the leaves of green I see a pair of moccasins trimmed with colored quills, moving with gentle tread toward me; and now a skirt of brown, and next a waist of red, half covered with tresses long and black that almost touch the ground. Another step, and now before me stands the maid, so close that I can see her bosom swell at every breath. A single rose with opening buds alone adorns her hair. Perfect she appears in make and mold of body and of limb. Her ruby lips stand just apart, exposing teeth of perfect make and white as snow. Her dark eyes full of soul beam forth surprise. She sees the newly made birch canoe—the boatman sees. Softly, on tiptoe, she turns about, moving noiselessly away. With struggling heart pressed in my throat, I step from out the boat upon the open shore, saying, "Boo-zhoo?"[1] (How do you do?) Then I said, with trembling voice, "Nic-con" (My friend). With modest smile, almost suppressed from her dark eyes, she greeted back, "Nic-con," with voice so winning and so bland my heart-strings vibrated with her tones. I now felt more at ease, for well I knew that she was flesh and blood, and understood the language of my tribe. Quietly and slowly I stepped toward her, when backward she withdrew, saying by look and deed, "Please, sir, no nearer come." I stayed my steps, and she again stood still, but watched me with suspicious eyes. Backward a space I stepped, as if to take the boat, and asked, "Kwaw-notch qua-zayns au-nish?" (Fair girl, who art thou?) Reluctantly and low, with downcast eyes, she said, "Lo-ni-daw." I then asked, "Au-ne-zhaw-kin?" (Where dost thou live?) "A-wass we-di" (Beyond the hill), she replied, pointing to an abrupt headland toward the rising sun. I then asked, "We-ni-aw ne-os-see-maw?" (Who is thy father?) Soberly she replied, "Ne-bou" (He is dead). "Do-dan ki bi-ma-dis ni-ji-ke?" (Dost thou live alone?) I asked. Shaking her head, she said, "Kaw" (No) "Nin-bi-ma-dis-nind o-gaw-she-maw" (I live with my mother). I then asked, "Nin-de a-i-an ni-mot-og kema a-we-mog?" (Have you any brothers or sisters?) Shaking her head, she replied, "Kaw." She then started off, walking faster and faster until she gained a run, passing out of sight among the trees. All now seemed like a dream, and as I reflected upon her presence, I well knew in my "o-daw" (heart) I never, never saw before so fair, so fair a one. Just as I stepped into "tchi-man" to cross se-bin, I glimpsed the snow-white deer coming up the stream, bounding toward me through bush and brake, through goldenrod, flags, and rushes tall. I now could hear and feel each pulsation of my heart. Nor will you think it strange when I tell you that the white deer, or albino deer, as white men call them, are very rare, and when seen in the forests among those of the natural color (red), the contrast is indeed striking. They have been called by our people, for time out of mind, "Mon-i-to-esh waw-be-waw-mawsh-kay-she" (The sacred deer of white); and we are taught from early childhood that if we should shoot at one, we would be sick, and if we should kill one, we would surely soon die. On came the sacred deer, to the very place where the maid had stood. Here he stopped; and, facing about, stood still, with

---

1. "Boo-zhoo" is without doubt a corruption of the French word, *bonjour* (good day or good morning). The word is generally used among all those tribes with which the French came in contact at an early day. It is regarded by most Indians as meaning, "Ta-ni ki dodam?" (How do you do?)

head erect. His antlers were triple-pronged and shaped alike, perfect in make, and white as snow. He stood so near that I could see his flashing eyes, see him wink, and hear him breathe. About his neck a wreath of flowers of red, white, and blue he wore. With nose upturned, and nostrils expanded wide, he snuffed to find what scented the morning air; then, with a piercing, whistling snort, he wheeled about, going like the wind, following on the maiden's track. Returning home, I told "nin-gaw" (my mother) all about my strange adventure. I opened wide the door of "nin-o-daw" (my heart), telling her she "kwaw-notch au-quay" (was the prettiest maid) I ever saw, and that she had awakened a strange admiration in my soul. She listened with marked attention, in wonder and surprise, asking me many strange questions, and most solemnly advising me to make no further attempts to solve the mystery of the mocking "ik-we" (maid) and the sacred deer of white, as she greatly feared some evil might befall me thereby.

However on the following day again I crossed the river, climbing the headland beyond which the maiden said her mother lived. Coming to an ancient trail, that plainly showed it had been lately used, I laid down near it, among the "anag-an-ask" (tall ferns), and there concealed myself, hoping the maid and deer might pass that way. Soon her voice I heard; but it sounded now more like the soft and tender notes of the mourning dove in the distance, and again more like the jay in imitation of the hawk, and again like the squirrel's sneezing, scolding bark, awakening the solitude with her varied chants and broken songs. Soon she came in sight, with hasty steps passing along the winding trail. But now, to my surprise, she wore a skirt of green and waist of white, holding in her hands some stalks of bloody cardinal in full bloom, which cast a halo of livelier green upon the foliage around. As she approached,—and I was intently gazing upon her slender form and steps so light and free,—she paused, and standing still near by me, backward looked along the trail. I said to my throbbing heart, "Be still!" then held my breath to drink her native beauty in. I faintly heard a rustling sound, as when the wind sweeps through the tall prairie grass, and soon saw, coming along the trail, the sacred deer of white, with bundles of rushes held between his spiky horns. Both passed by, leaving me unobserved.

Squirrels red, black, and gray came following on the trail, as though they sought the woodland maid to see. Meditating there awhile, I arose, recalling to mind the advice of "nin-gaw" (my mother) not to pursue the mocking "ik-we" (maid). With grave misgivings in "nin-o-daw" (my heart), I followed down the trail until I reached a valley deep below, where underbrush almost concealed a wigwam tent of colored rushes made, that glistened like the rainbow among the trees; while all about hung mats of different shades, shapes, and sizes, adorned with various colored quills and feathers.

Nearing, on tiptoe, the secluded spot, all was silent as the grave. No sound I heard, except the babbling brook close by. But all at once there burst upon my listening ears a whistling snort that made the welkin ring. I shuddered like a child that hears a panther scream. Quickly I turned around, and there before me stood the sacred deer of white, stamping his feet to frighten me away. Cautiously I stepped up to the rainbow-colored tent, and there listening awhile, heard some one in a whisper say, "Pe-naw! Pe-naw!" (Hark! Hark!) No other sound I heard within. Cautiously as the mousing cat I walked around the tent, but found no place to enter in. At length with trembling hand I pulled a cord that I thought might be the latch-string of some matting door, when lo! to my surprise, all sides of the wigwam rolled up in a scroll! and there, in open, broad daylight, before me sat the maiden and her mother!

They laid aside their braid, and gazed at me as though I had no business there; and so I felt, but said as pleasantly as possible for an intruder in such a fix, "Boo-zhoo-nic-con-og?" (How do you do, my friends?) Both timidly responded, with speech suppressed, "Boo-zhoo-nic-con." Rising to her feet, the mother said, "Pin-di-gayn" (Come in). I stepped inside; so did the deer, and stood beside the maid, with his nose upon her shoulder laid. The mother picked up a fancy mat, placing it upon the ground beside me. I said, "Ne-gwetch" (Thanks), and reclined upon it. She then reached above her head and pulled a cord; the matting scrolls unrolled, and down they came, enclosing us on every side. At first it seemed as if the shades of night were coming on; but soon, more like the dawn of day, the light came on apace, till all within the room was plainly to be seen. The mother had a queenly step and royal mien, but the many furrows in her cheeks most plainly told they had been deepened by many a flood of tears. At length the maid, with modest smile almost concealed, spoke out, and said, "Ne-ge-wob ke-waw-waw pe-tchi-maw-go se-be" (I saw you at the river yesterday). I replied, "Ka-ge-te" (Truly so). The mother, with a curious smile, almost suppressed, now asked, "We-i-ki?" (Who art thou?) "Pokagon," I replied. She then asked, "Waw kaw-in Ogi-maw Pokagon Pottawattamie?" (What! not old Chief Pokagon of the Pottawattamies?)

I replied, "Kaw o-daw-en-guis" (No, I am his son). "Au-nish! (What!) not young Simaw?" I answered, "Ne-ween" (I am he). Then said, "Did you know Ne-os-see-maw (my father)?" Anxiously she inquired, "Au-nish! Po-ka-gon au-ke-wa-she Le-o-pold smo-ke-mon?" (What! not the son of Chief Pokagon—Leopold, as white men called him?) "Ae" (Yes), I said. She then replied, "Ke-au-yaw kitch-ti-wa-wis au-nish-naw-be—o-gi-maw" (He was a noble man and chief). "Win-sa-gi-i-we—man-i-tan ba-ta-do-dan" (He loved right and hated wrong). "Nin wid-i-ge-ma-gan (my husband) was chief under him many, many years; they went together to see the great white chief at Washington." She then advanced a step toward me, saying, "Nind an-am-i-et-ä-waw ki sa-nagise kwi-wi-sens (Bless you, my dear boy), Simaw! I have swung you in tik-in-a-gan (hammock), and carried you on nin-pik-wan (my back) time and time again. Bless you! I lived with your o-gaw-she-maw when you were born. And you are my boy, Simaw. The Great Spirit bless you. Does ke-o-gaw-she-maw (your mother) yet live?" "Ae, nan-ge-ka" (Yes, certainly), I replied. "Au-ne-zhaw?" (Where?) she asked. "Just across the great Sebe," I replied. The maiden now drew near, followed by the deer, and stood beside her mother. She gave me the most winsome smile I ever saw. The mother saw it, too, and said, "Ma-bamki-da-nis Lo-ni-daw" (This is my daughter Lonidaw). Again she smiled, more winsome than before. A strange feeling came over me. I felt a sacred thrill of joy, unknown before, rush through my frame, reaching my very soul; to which my heart responding said, "The maid is surely mine." The mother again asked: "And do you really mean to say your o-gaw-she-maw still lives?" I replied, "Ka-ge-ta maw-got!" (It is surely so!) "Au-nish! (What!) Ka-law-na Po-ka-gon?" "Ae; that's my mother's name by Christian rule and law." Statue-like she stood, finally saying, "Neen-ke-no-bo shong-we ne-go-twos-we! (I was sure she died fifteen years ago!) And yet she lives? Au-to-yaw? (Is it possible?) I was left nin-gi-wis (an orphan) at my birth; your mother's mother brought me up. Ae, your o-gaw-she-maw and I nursed and played with your no-ko-miss (grandmother) together; we slept on oni-ka-mag (her arms) together; were carried on odi-niman-gan (her shoulders) together; swung from wa-nak'-ong (tree top) in her hammock together; ba-pine-nim gaie maw-win mam-awi (rejoiced and wept together). And you do say she is still alive, and ni-be-win (camping) just across the Sebe?" "Ae," I said, "but we may leave for home wa-bang (tomorrow)." She then exclaimed, "Ne-dge-bawn! (my soul!) ne-gaw-wob-yaw ne-gon-ke-sus

(I must see her before the sun goes down). Ke-na-wind-ke-win ne-go-ting (We will go home with you at once)." "All right," I said, "but ne-tche-maw-nes-on (my boat is small), and will float pa-zhig (but one)." "Well, then," said she, with a smile, "Lo-da haw-yea-ne (Loda and I) will bim-a-daga a-jaw-aona (swim across)." She then said, "Lo-da, get ne-waw-bo-yon (my blanket) and a ball of twine." The blanket was brought, and tenderly thrown over her head and shoulders. I started homeward, followed by the mother and the maid, and the deer brought up the rear.

III

O n reaching the boat, launched by the river's shore, Lonidaw
handed her mother the ball of twine which she had brought.
She quickly tied the cord to the bow of the boat, carefully got in, and
while Lonidaw held the ball, she pushed out into the stream. I now
first knew why the twine was brought. The maid and I now left alone,
with none to hear except the deer, our words were very few and simple;
but our thoughts were many, and filled with eloquence. Soon the
mother reached the other shore, and with her hand a motion made for
Lonidaw to wind up the cord. In her nimble hands the ball spun like
a top; the boat returning, as if impelled by some unseen power divine,
soon reached our landing-place. I now reached for the maiden's hand
to help her into the boat. The watchful deer sprang forward, as if to
help her too; but quick as "she-gos-see" (the weasel) she bounded in
herself, handed me the ball, grasped the oar, and like "wa-bi-si" (the
swan) pushed out into the stream.

The deer gave one whistling, snorting snuff, then bounded twenty
feet or more into the stream, swimming close behind the boat until it
reached the other shore. Pulling back the boat with the cord, soon I
crossed and joined them on the other side. Nearing our wigwam summer
home, our dog, old Maw-kaw, met us on the trail, with hair along his
back upturned, and threatening growl, came near the maid, and nosed
her hand. The mother stopped, and standing still, she asked, "Ne-daw-
yo-em-e-waw-au-nish?" (Is that your dog?) "Ae," I replied. She then
said, "I fear Maw-mawsh-kay-she saw au-ni-moosh" (the deer will kill
him). "Yaw-kaw" (O, no), I said, "he is maw-in-gawn au-ni-moosh (a
wolf dog), and has killed many a deer and wolf." While yet I spoke, the
deer sprang at the dog as fiercely as the mountain "pe-zhen" (lynx) that
guards her young, striking him with his three-pronged antlers square in
the breast; and as he turned to run, gave him another cruel punch full
in the rear, which sent him yelping into the house. My mother heard
the fearful yells, and thought perhaps "me-she-be-she" (a panther) had
pounced upon the dog, and quickly shut to the door. I opened it, and
we three, without a word, walked into the room. She gazed at them in
wonder and surprise, thinking perhaps it might be that I had caught the
maiden mocking spirit of the woods beyond the river, with some other
being of her kind, together with the sacred deer of white, that now

stood just outside the open door, with head drooped low, as if expecting to give the skulking dog another punch. Fearing the deer might venture in, quickly I shut to the door, saying, "O-gaw-she-maw me de-mo-gay?" (Do you know this old lady?) She gazed at her with the most inquiring look I ever saw, then rushed into her arms, exclaiming, "My dear Ko-bun-da!" while the stranger answered back, "My dear Ka-law-na! my dear Ka-law-na, are we dreaming, or are we both awake?" Unclasping their embrace, my mother threw her arms about the daughter's neck, while her mother threw hers around mine, "odg-in-di-win" (kissing) us as if we were but little children. Then both sat down and wept with joy together.

Lonidaw and I also wept, to see them weep. At last, looking upward through her tears, my mother said, "Ko-bun-da (Do tell me) where you have been, and all about it; for I was told, time and time again, that you perished in mit-a-gog (the woods) near Ni-jo-de sa-ga-ig-an-og (Twin Lakes),[1] near Me-no-mi-nee village, in trying to hide from the

---

1. In an article read before the Indiana Historical Society of South Bend, by Daniel Mc Donald, editor of the Plymouth *Democrat,* a newspaper published at Plymouth, Ind., near where the old Indian village was located, appears the following history: Several treaties between the United States and different bands of the Pottawattamies were made in northern Indiana, whereby they were to leave the State within two years and go on a reservation to be provided for them west of the Mississippi River; but when the time arrived, many of them, especially the Me-no-mi-nee band, refused to leave because Me-no-mi-nee, their chief, had not and would not sign any treaty to sell their land and remove West. David Wallace, father of General Lew Wallace, author of "Ben Hur," was governor of Indiana at that time, and he, on complaint of white settlers who coveted the Indian lands, issued an order in August, 1838, that they should be removed from the State at once.

The order was executed by General Tipton, who marched to the Indian village, and surrounded it with a body of soldiers before the Indians had any knowledge of the military move whatever. Some were taken prisoners in their church, where they had assembled by deception of spies sent out for that purpose, while others were taken in Me-no-mi-nee village and the surrounding country. On the next day after they were taken prisoners, they were allowed to hold a meeting in their little graveyard, a short distance from their village, at which a final farewell of the dead was taken, as they were to leave the following morning, never to return. Weeping and wailing, which was confined to a few at first, became general, and they were compelled by the soldiers to leave the yard. In solemn reverence, they turned their weeping faces from the sleeping dead, never to look upon the graves of their kindred again.

The next day, Sept. 2. 1838, orders were given to move; and at once nearly one thousand men, women, and children, with broken hearts and tearful eyes, took up the line of march for their far Western home.

United States troops at the time they so shamefully captured the most of our people, forcing them toward the setting gis-is (sun) beyond the great river."

We all reclined on our blankets to listen to her story. She began: "On the morning of that sad day at Twin Lakes, of which you speak, Sin-a-gaw, my husband, told me that a stranger had been around, informing all the Au-nish-naw-bay-og (Indians) that our Christian priest wished all the tribe to meet him at Au-naw-ma-we gaw-ming (wigwam church), and desired me to go with him. But being au-kee-zee (sick), I remained at home. He faithfully promised me he would be back by the middle of the afternoon; but night came on, and neither he nor any of those I had seen going to church in the morning had yet returned. I felt impressed, deep down in my heart, that something awful had happened. As I was sadly brooding over my thoughts, the door was wide open flung, and in came a little boy of the white race, who was a playmate of au-nish-naw-be o-nid-gan-is (Indian children), and who loved Sin-a-gaw, my husband, and me. As he rushed into our wigwam, all out of breath, he was crying, 'Murder! murder! murder! O dear, dear!' He could say no more, falling exhausted on the floor. In a few moments he raised up, and stammered out, 'O dear, dear! Lots and lots of white men I never seed before, all dressed in blue, have got all the Injuns in the church tied together with big strings, like ponies, and are going to kill all of um. O dear, dear! Do run quick and hide!' I said, 'Hold on, Skiney. Do tell me if you saw Sin-a-gaw among them?' He replied, 'O dear! Yes, me did; and me hear somebody say, "Skiney, come here," and it was Sin-a-gaw. And he talk low, and say to tell you to hide in the big woods a few days, then go to the old Ot-ta-wa trapper's wigwam, and if he not get killed, me by he get loose and find you. Do run quick! Dear, dear, they will get us! Me do wish I could kill um all.' I gathered up what few clothes I had and left our home, never to return. I ran across the great trail to your wigwam; no one was there. I heard several going past on the run. I heard some one speak in a heavy voice. It was Go-bo. I never heard him talk excited before. He said the whole country was alive with white warriors catching Au-nish-naw-bay-og,

---

Official reports show that one hundred and fifty were missing when they arrived at their reservation, the most of whom died on their journey. My father, Chief Leopold Pokagon, by special contract with the government for himself and his band, were to be permitted to remain in Michigan; yet many of his band, regardless of the agreement, were taken and hurried off with the rest.

to kill or drive them toward the setting sun. All doubts of Skiney's story were now removed. I ran north into a desolate swamp, which I had been taught from infancy was the home of jin-awe (rattlesnakes) and maw-in-gwan-og (wolves), and there hid myself in the hollow of a fallen sycamore tree. It was an awful ne-tchi-wad te-be-kut (stormy night); wolves howled in the distance, as if following on my track; me-she-be-she (a panther) near by me screamed like a woman in dire distress. In the morning Loda, that girl, was born! I there remained one week, keeping aw-be-non-tchi (the infant) wrapped up as best I could. On the morning of the seventh sun I started northward to find the old trapper. I was weak and hungry, as all I had eaten while there was a small piece of jerked venison not larger than my hand, and a few beechnuts; but, thanks to the Great Spirit, I found in my journey an o-me-me (a young pigeon) so fat it could not fly. I sat down on a log and ate it raw. It tasted good, and gave me strength. In four days I reached the old trapper's wigwam, where myself and child were kindly cared for. I there first learned the fate of my people, and was told tchi ki das-sos (that you were trapped) in the church with many others, and driven far westward.

"Late in wintertime my husband returned, and found me and our little one. He had traveled on foot and alone across the great plains from far beyond the 'father of waters,' and was so broken down in health and spirits that he seemed all unlike himself. He sought to gain new life by drinking 'fire-water' more and more; but alas, in a few years it consumed him, and he faded and fell, as fall the leaves in autumn time. I have lived since then among the Ottawas up the great Sebe. I learned of them to do all kinds of bark and braid work, by which Loda and I have supported ourselves. Although she came to me in the most desolate wilderness of sorrow, yet she has been my only joy and hope. I often think the circumstances under which she was born in the swamp, amid the screams of birds of prey, and the cries of beasts, and songs of singing birds, had much to do with her wonderful gifts. She can imitate all creatures from the mouse to the elk, from the bee to the swan."

As she said these last words, Lonidaw smiled on me, and placing one hand over "nin o-daw" (her heart), said, "E-we-nin" (That's me). We two listened until after midnight to their strange stories of sunshine and of storm. I then engaged the attention of the beautiful girl, as I was indeed anxious to have many things explained that were hidden in mystery. I inquired for what reason she and her mother were camping across the Sebe? She replied, "We are making mats and rugs to sell to white people. The finest flags and rushes we have ever found grow on wau-bawsh-ko-ke an-a-kan-nash (a marsh) close by." I then inquired why it was she always went up and never down the stream. "Well," said she, "in gathering flags and rushes for our work, I went up Sebe on account of the beautiful scenery along the shore, and also that my deer might have good feeding grounds; but on returning home with my flags and rushes I always take another course along the old trail, which is much nearer."

I now inquired where she got the snow-white deer. "I will tell you all about that," she replied. "Some four years ago, while I was passing through the woods, I affrighted ki nin-ge suc-see (the mother deer) by the trailside, which ran away and left o-kit-a-ga-kons (her fawn) when first born. It mistook me for its mother. I tried to drive it back; still it continued to follow me. I then tried to run away from it, but could not, and it followed me home. We raised it on pony's milk," said she, "and you may think it strange, but if I pet aw-es-si (any animal) or human kind in the presence of that deer, he will pitch at them with all his might. In fact, he drove from our camp the pony that had nursed him, because I sometimes petted her."

I said, "He must love you," "Yes," she said, "I think he does; and although he has never told ki-sa-gia (his love) in words, yet by his acts he has shown the secret of his heart; and if you had taken my hand last night, as you attempted to do, to help me into tchi-man (the boat), I believe, as I live, he would have served you as he did ki an-i-mos (your dog) a short time after." I then asked, "What did your mother and you think yesterday, when I came to your wigwam and through mistake let broad daylight in upon you?" She answered, "We were surprised, but felt quite safe, from the fact that the deer followed you in, taking his place by my side. We well knew if you undertook to do us harm, you would encounter ki-esh-kan-og (his antlers) in a manner you did not expect." She further said, "When you met me at se-bin (the river) the morning before, for the first time, I felt mistrustful of you, and would have left at once, only I expected my deer every moment, as he was feeding just below; but as he did not come on, as I expected, I hastened away; but he overtook me before I reached the marsh." With some reluctance I now asked, "What did you tell your mother about me on your return home?" "Ek-waw, ek-waw! (Well, well!)" said she, with a curious smile, "I told her I met osh-ki-naw-we (a young man) a-gam-ing Se-be (near the river's shore) a-gwi-win-on dow-an o-gi-maw (dressed like a chief), gi-git mo-ja-gis-sin-on i-go (and he spoke kindly to me), ma-kaw tchi min-bim ib-a-to (but that I ran away and left him); and after I had gotten away began to wish I had stayed longer, and learned more about him, for he could speak the Ottawa and Pottawattamie o-daw-naw-naw (tongue)." "Well, what did ki o-gaw sha-maw ik-kit (your mother say)?" "She said, 'You did kit-chi (right), Loda, mis-so-ke pa-was (keep away) from such nidg au-nish-nobe-og (fellows); ne-sa-ge-ze ke-te-mesh-ke mau-tchi osh-kee-maw-waw (no doubt he is a drinking, lazy, bad young man).'"

We all talked on and on, regardless of night or time, until interrupted by harsh gratings on the door, which, with its squeaking wail, wide open flung, followed by the deer, which put his fore feet just inside the door, and there stood still. Fearing his jealous heart, I quickly left Lonidaw's side, while she sprang to his head. Pressing her hands against his face, she said, "I-ja-pik-wan, i-ja-pik-wan (Go back, go back), mau-tchi maw-mawsh-ka-she (bad deer); *i-ja-pik-wan, i-ja-pik-wan* (go back, go back)." He backed outside the open door; and she, too, went out. Her mother said, "Step to the door, and see them play," and we did so. The deer would run in circles swift about her, then turning square about, rush straight toward her, dropping on his knees in front of her, and rubbing his chin on the ground by a rolling motion to and fro with his neck and head; then, like a purring cat, roll over, and springing to his feet, like a young dog would run round and round the old wigwam, stopping just in sight now and then, as if trying to play hide-and-seek with her. At last he walked boldly up to her, and she placed her arm over his neck and shoulders, patting him under the neck and chin, which he seemed to enjoy, with eyes half closed as if almost asleep. I will not admit that I was jealous of the deer, but most humbly confess that I *did* covet the attention he received.

IV

To our surprise it was late in the forenoon. Mother hastily prepared our simple woodland meal of "she-shep," "ke-gon," and "me-daw-min" (duck, fish, and corn), a right royal meal for kindred souls who had gone supperless all night. While eating, our guests informed us they expected "Au-ke-wa-ze," the old Ottawa trapper, down the Sebe during the day to take them home; as he had promised, when he brought them there, to be back "ne-tawn" "to-bik-ke-zes" (the first full moon) in that month. After breakfast we all went down to the river's shore to keep watch for the old trapper. About noon we caught sight of his long birch canoe rounding the river's bend far up the stream. The old man was singing in his mother tongue, while bending to the oars with all his might. In front of him, on his knees, was a little boy with head erect, as if steering for some object far down the stream. On reaching a point opposite where we sat, the maid and her mother rising to their feet, waved their hands. The boat at once turned in midstream, landing on the beach close beside us. The old man and little boy both chimed out, "Boo-zhoo-nic-con-og?" and both leaped from the boat. The old man seized Lonidaw's hand, while her lips and the little boy's together met; after which her mother kissed the lad, and shook the old man's hand. He was now introduced to us as "o-me-shaw-way-e-maw" (uncle) Kaw-be-naw, their old "ji-ki-we" (friend), the Ottawa trapper. After saluting mother and me with a nod of the head, he took great pride in telling us the little boy was only "me-tos-we" (ten) years old, and that he was "ne-daw-niss-esh ne-daw-niss" (his daughter's daughter's) youngest child, "Non-nee-on-son" (little Nonnee). The aged man was rudely dressed in old-time Indian style, and judging from his long, gray hair, and the many wrinkles in his face, eighty years or more had left their impress there. Yet he was straight, tall, and active as a youth. His teeth were of perfect make, and white as snow. The boy wore cap and feathers trimmed in white and red, with a tanned fawn-skin about his hips, reaching to his knees. Its star-like spots of pure white, scattered through the light red hair, appeared in perfect harmony with his childlike face and acts of innocence.

We urged the old man to stay with us all night and start back in the morning. He did not favor the plan, until Lonidaw told him "nin-o-gaw-she-maw" (my mother) was an old playmate of "nin-o-gaw-she-maw" (her mother), and that each had supposed the other dead until the day before. Silently a while he stood and eyed us with suspicious looks; then gazing at his shadow, and then at the sun, slowly said, "Mano, ae (well, yes), nind in-en-da nin-gash-ki-ton (I suppose I can stay), but would like to load bin-ish te-be-cut (up tonight) so as to start gi-gi ke-sus wau-bung (with the sun tomorrow morning)." The girl and her mother assured him that they could do as he desired. He then took out of the boat a string of ducks and some fish, which he threw on the shore, saying, "Well, then, if we must stay all night, let us have we-kau-de-win (a feast)." He then picked up his bow (as long as he was tall), loosened the strings, and placed it back into the boat again across a pair of young deer horns. I said, "I see you have killed a deer, where is he?" "Io" (Oh), he replied, "they are nin-to-tem (my mascot)," pointing to the deer that just came to the shore. "They are nind bi-bon esh-kan-og (his last year's horns). Loda mi-gi-we (gave them to me). Ne zhawg (I always) keep them in my boat; they bring pa-pe-we-win (good luck)." While I was considering how the deer might feel toward the queer old man and little lad, he picked up the ducks and fish and threw them across the shoulders of the deer, saying, "You carry them, ge-te gaw-we-win-og (old jealousy)." Then turning to Lonidaw, he asked, "Has he nit-a-ga o-ma" (killed anybody here)? Quickly the answer came, "He never killed anybody here, or elsewhere, as I know of." "Io, kaw (Oh, no)," he said; "I can not say he has, but ash-ki smo-ke-mon (a young white man) told me the other day that he saw you picking nis-sim-in-og (berries), when he was a little ki-wash-kwe-bi (boozy), and while trying to shake hands with you, ke-pik-i-ke nin o-dib (he pitched him headlong) into maw-tchi (cruel) patch of wau kau-tay mis-kou-min-og (blackberry briar bushes), broke his o-mo-dai (jug), and almost broke his o-kaw-gun (neck)."

We now started up the terrace trail in double file, rounding the headland for the wigwam, my mother and her old-time friend in the lead, followed by Lonidaw and the deer, while the old man and I brought up the rear. The boy, like a butterfly, flitted about, first on one side and then the other, picking the fairest flowers and giving them to Lonidaw, who received them with as much grace and good-will as a white belle receives diamonds from her lover.

As we walked along, the old man began to tell me what a wonderful child Loda had always been, and how she was born in "mash-kig" (a swamp) while "kiga" (her mother) was hiding away from the United States troops, who were on "mi-gad swin mi-kan" (the war-path); and that she was carried by her starving mother fifty miles or more through tangled "ki-bins" (brush) and over high hills and through valleys deep and wild to his wigwam, when she was but a few days old; and that Nature had taught her the language of "awessi gaie bineshi (beasts and birds), so that she could talk and sing with them. "And," said he, "if she would make use of her wonderful min-i-gowin (gifts), she could nish-iwe min-a-wa (kill more) game than a dozen old hunters. When she was no larger than Non-nee-on-son, I have seen assemble at her alluring call, flocks of me-zhe-say-wog (turkeys), pe-na-wog (partridges), she-shep-og (ducks), and all kinds of singing be-nesh-i (birds); and hunters in the country where she lived, when game in plenty could be found, would always say, 'Loda must have passed along this way.' I have tried many times to have her call beasts and birds together for me to shoot, but she would always say, with a shake of her head, 'Kaw, kaw (No, no); I can not tell them ni-kan-niss (I am their friend), and while they trust in Loda, have you shoot them down. I hate gin-big (the snake), that charms to kill.'"

He paused a while and then said, "She and her mother can make anything they desire out of ke-ki-we-on, an-ak an-ashk, mash-kos-o, wi-gwas-si, and ko-go-bi-we (flags, rushes, sweet-grass, birch bark, and porcupine quills), and stain them in all the colors of nag-we-i-ab (the rainbow)." He finally asked, "Have you seen her shoot ki mit-i-gwab a-chi mit-i-gwan-wi (her bow and arrow)?" I replied that I had not. "Osh-kee-maw (Young man)," he said, "I taught tchi ikwe-sens (that girl) how to hold and bend mit-i-gwab (the bow); she can send aw-tus (an arrow) straight as sight."

He then asked, "Can you talk smo-ke-mon talk?" I informed him that I had recently returned from Twinsburg Academy in Ohio, where I had studied smo-ke-mon (the white man's) language for three years, and that during all that time I had only seen two Indians, Petoskey and Blackbird[2] of the Traverse Bay region in Michigan. He then said, pointing to little Nonnee, "That kwi-wi-sens (boy) is my tur-ket-er with smo-ke-mon. He has been with Sketer, a smo-ke-mon boy, and can say all the smo-ke-mon words." He then called out, "Non-nee, come here." The boy came, and walked beside us. "Now," said the old

---

2. Petoskey, referred to, was one of the Petoskey family now residing in the city of Petoskey, Mich., whose name the city bears. Blackbird, A. J., still resides at Harbor Springs, Mich. He is about eighty years old; was postmaster of that place for several years, and is author of a book entitled, "The History of the Ottawa and Chippewa Indians of Michigan." He is a very remarkable man.

man, "you ask ki ga-gwed-wewin (him questions) like a smo-ke-mon, and he will answer like a smo-ke-mon." So I said, "Nonnee, where do you live?" "Me by I guess here," he said, holding his hand over his breast. I then said, "But I want to know where—in wa-a-bi-nas (what place)?" "Guess me by in the woods," he said. "But where," I asked. Pointing up the river, he said, "Guess me by dat way." "But how was-sa a-maw (far from here)?" He answered, "Guess me by one day, if not wind; if wind, me by two days." I then asked, "Where are you going?" "Guess me by where granddad goes, me goes." "When did you leave home?" "Guess me by when sun start, we start." I then said, "How long ago was it when you first saw your granddad?" He began to laugh as though it was a foolish question, and said, "Me guess me by me neber seed him first; always me hab seed him." "How old are you, my boy?" "I guess dat me by me can't tell dat. No tink time me did not lib." At each answer the old man would eye the boy, making silent motions with his lips as the boy did, at the close of each answer, exclaiming, "Me-no, me-no (Good, good);" and in conclusion said, "Can you talk smo-ke-mon like that?" Not wishing faith lost in the boy's knowledge of English, I said, "No, not like that."

On arriving at the wigwam, the old man took one of the ducks, and hanging it up by a string to a limb of a tree, said, "Now, quay-zaynes (my girl), I want you and osh-kee-maw-waw (this young man) to shoot at that duck, and see which one of you can first cut the string and bring it down." She stepped quietly up to the old man, and putting her arms about his neck, whispered something in his ears I could not hear, but overheard him say, "How foolish! you ought to be proud of it. When I brought you here a few moons ago, you were quay-zaynes-on-son (a small girl), but now you are mi-she au-quaw (big woman)." So saying, he took the duck and handed it to her, as if perplexed, saying, "Here, take it, pick it, dress and cook it for the feast." While she yet held gi-shib (the duck) in one hand, the boy stepped up to her, and taking her by the other hand, said, "O, dear Loda, I thought all the way down the river, what a nice time me and you would have again running, jumping, and playing with waw-mawsh-kay-she. Come, now; do let us have a keel and race." Loda left at once, saying, "I must help prepare the feast." The old man looked at me with a curious grin, saying, "It does seem too bad Loda has no time to play with Non-nee-on-son."

While the women were preparing the big feast, the old man and I reclined in the shade of "mit-tig" (the woods) in true native style. I said, "Ko-bun-da, my mother's childhood friend, tells her that you were acquainted with nin-gaw (my father), Leopold Pokagon, in his lifetime." "Ae," he replied, "I well knew O-gi-maw (Chief) Pokagon, long, long time ago. And is it possible you are his son?" "I am. He died when I was a little boy, about the size of Nonnee." "Ae; young man, I knew him well; he was a noble man, perfect chief. He loved his people as he loved himself. I well now recall seeing him with Chiefs Me-nom-e-ne, Blackwolf, Ben-neck, and Sin-a-gaw (Loda's father),—all of those renowned chiefs on pony-back in Me-nom-e-ne village, starting off to see the great father of the United States at Washington, who had sent for them to come and see him. They were all dressed in ornamented buckskin, wearing fine, beaded moccasins, and wi-wak-wan-og (caps) trimmed with mi-gi-si mi-gwan-og (eagle feathers). They left just as the forest leaves were turning mis-kwa (red), and were gone all pe-boon (winter), coming back me-nou-kaw-me (in the spring) when the forest was getting o-zhaw-wash-kwa (green). I remember well ke-zhe-gut (the day) they came home. Mon-do-te-be-cut (That night) all the aw-nish-naw-by-og (Indian men) met at our church; they make gi-git-owin-og (speeches), and tell us they ride ponies as far as Wheeling, O., and leave them there all winter with some white men. There they get into a big wagon drawn ne-win mis-ta-tim (by four horses), and rode night and day to Baltimore; from there they take monster wagon drawn on iron poles, with fire and smoke, to Washington.[3] They tell us what great things they see among the white men, and how the great white chief gave them beds, and fed them all winter, feasting all the time; and how he wanted to buy our aki (land) for his own people. But they said they would not sell o-aki (our land), and leave ke-win-og (our homes) and tchi-be-gam-ig (the graves) of os-see-mowg and o-gaw-she-maw (our fathers and mothers), and go beyond mi-che-se-pe (the great river). We all rejoiced, and spat our hands, shouting, 'Me-no! me-no! me-no!' (Good! good! good!)

"But when tau-gwan-gee (fall time) came again, Chief Pepper and Chief Morgan, both war chiefs of the white people, came among us on horseback, dressed fine, and talk big, telling us the great father at Washington had bought all our land, and that we all must leave, and

3. At the time referred to, when my father went to Washington, the first railroad he reached was at Baltimore. He was nearly three weeks on the way. Thirty years after, I went over nearly the same route by rail, reaching there in less than two days.

go toward the setting sun to a strange land. We knew we had not sold our land, and refused to go away to an unknown au-kee (land). In a few days a great many smo-ke-mon came on the war-path, all dressed in we-binguaw (blue) with do-ta a-saw-aw-jo-ni-id (buttons of gold), armed with guns and bayonets; and all our people that they could catch, they forced away to Kansas, across the great plains. Some they drove like cattle, and others they tied like sheep for market, and carried them in wagons. Great many died on the way, and were eaten by win-an-geg (vultures) and by maw-in-gwan-og (wolves). I do not like to talk about it; nin o-daw (my heart) gets sad! You ought to hear Loda's mother tell of man-esi-win (the want) and kash-ken dam-i-de-win (the sorrow of her heart) which she endured, and——"

Here we were interrupted by a childlike cry, screaming "paw-kaw, paw-kaw, paw-kaw (whoa, whoa, whoa)." Springing to our feet, to our surprise we saw the deer running around the wigwam, with the boy astride like the show monkey and the pony in the ring; his fawn-skin skirt and cap were flying in the wind behind, while he was clinging on for his dear life, with all his might. The women heard the fearful scream, and rushed outdoors, Lonidaw in advance, all exclaiming, "Au-to-yo! Au-to-yo! Au-to-yo!" (expressions of great surprise). The deer on seeing Loda, broke his run into a trot, and to her came and stopped. The boy fell naked into her arms, while her mother picked up his cap and skirt and put them on again. The maiden laughed most heartily, petting the lad until he too began to laugh in unison with her, while tears were streaming down his cheeks. The little boy, in his grief, would only say "mau-tchi suc-see, mau-tchi suc-see (bad deer, bad deer)."

Supper being now announced, we all reclined around the pots of steaming ko-pin-yak,[4] fish, and ducks. No king or courtier, in palace bred, with all his pomp and show of tables, chairs, and dishes, could have more enjoyed his meal.

---

4. "Ko-pin-yak," the tuberous roots of a kind of flag that grows along streams and lakes, used as food by many tribes of Indians. In preparing it for use, a hole was dug in the ground five or six feet deep and about the same in width. In the bottom of this hole, stones were placed, and fire built thereon until they were heated nearly red-hot. Wet moss was then placed over them, on top of which five or six bushels of these tubers were placed, over which was spread more moss nearly a foot thick. Several days were required to cook them properly, the stones being reheated once each day, removing the tubers for that purpose. When fully prepared according to custom, they were cut in slices and dried for future use. Thus an article unfit to eat raw, was made very nutritious and palatable.

After supper we all crossed the river in the old man's boat, followed by the deer, to the maiden's and her mother's camping grounds.

In haste we packed their tent and goods into the boat, returning to our landing-place. As soon as the women and myself had gone ashore and started on our way, the old man spoke out and said, "Oshki ogimaw (Young chief), hold on; step this way." I did so. No sooner had the women gone out of sight, than he opened a long box of "anibi-wanak" (elm bark), in which was placed, apparently with much care, two bows of pure white hickory, and many arrows, feathered white and red, of the finest make I ever saw. The old man, smiling, said, "These belong to Loda." "Did you make them?" I asked. "Io, kaw (O, no)," he said, "she made them all with her nimble hands, and stained and feathered them. She can use mo-ko'-man (knife) with greater skill than any que-we-zayns (boy) I ever saw. That is not all; she can go-gi and bim-a-da-ga (dive and swim) like she-sheb (a duck)."

Just then I heard a cry: "Au-mon-og! au-mon-og! au-mon-og!" (Bumblebees! bumblebees! bumblebees!) and there came the boy running and keeling down the bank, brushing his head with both hands. The old man quickly handed him "o-mo-da-i" (a jug), saying, "Here, take this, there is plenty of ni-bish (water) in it. Go and get their si-sib-a-kwat (honey)." He hurried back up the bank with the jug, and we followed him. Coming to a chunk of broken wood, he set the jug down beside it, turned the chunk over, and ran away from it. The bees swarmed out in great numbers; but to my surprise, whenever they came near the mouth of the jug, they would drop one by one into it until all were drowned. The boy then picked up the nest, comb and all, and taking a section of the cells that were filled with honey, placed the brood-comb back into the nest again. After we had eaten the honey, I said, "Uncle Kaw-be-naw, are all bumblebees such fools as that?" He replied, "Yes, they are; but I can not say that they are any greater gaw-an-a-di-sid (fools) than humankind, who from the same nozzle guzzle down awsh-kon-tay ne-besh (fire-water) that leads them down to shay-ni-bo-win (shame and death)." Then, looking thoughtfully a few moments, he said, "I have some time since come to son-gi-ton (the conclusion) that we could only excuse the bees for these foolish acts on the ground that all smo-ke-mon jugs are possessed with mau-tchi mon-i-to (the devil)!"

V

Having slept none the previous night, as the sun went down, we all wrapped our blankets about us, and lay down to sleep. At midnight's hour, the old man shook my arm, saying, "Ke-baw-win?" (Are you asleep?) "Yes," I replied, "until you shook me." He sighed, and then said, "Young chief, I can not understand how one of all our race can sleep when he recalls how awsh-kon-tay ne-besh (firewater), that alluring jan-gend-ji-ged (enemy) brought among us by the whites, is destroying kwi-wi-zens and osh-kin-äw-e (our boys and young men), as well as ak-i-wes-i (our old men), and laying waste qua-notch win (the fairest) of ki au-kee (our land). When a child you must have seen Ka-zell,[1] o-dan-is-san (the daughter) of Chief O-she-a-be, sometimes called by white men, Ben-neck, one of the chiefs of whom I spoke that visited Washington with ki nos-se (your father). That old chief and his wife died when Ka-zell was but twelve years old. They left her at the Catholic school near South Bend, Ind. Twelve thousand dollars fell to her from her father's estate. At the tender age of fourteen, she gave her o-daw (heart) and o-nind-ji-maw (hand) to a French Indian. He was much older than she, and a fine looking fellow; but in less than five years he squandered all O jo-ni-a (her money), drinking fire-water. He abused her most shamefully. It broke her young, confiding o-de-i-ma (heart); the sunshine in nish-kin-ma (her face) went out; her merry ba-pi-win (laugh) no more was heard; her osh-kin-jig-o-mag (eyes) grew dim; her on-o-wa-mag (cheeks) grew pale; her long raven wi-nis-is-si-mag (hair), reaching to au-kee (the ground), fell off; her tchi-tchag (soul) in a-bit-a-tib-i-kad (the midnight) of kash-ken-dam (sorrow wept). One kind act alone her drunken o-no-be-mi-na (husband) did for her: nis-sa-bawe (he drowned himself)! It does pain nin o-daw (my heart), when I consider that there is not one chance in go-twock (one hundred) for Loda, or any of our girls, to marry a young man of their tribe or people, who will not get drunk and abuse them! Do think of it!

---

1. Ka-zell, the chief's daughter referred to, had many warm admirers among young white men near Tippecanoe, Ind., where her father lived, who sought her hand in marriage; all of whom she rejected. One of them was so infuriated by her determination not to marry him that he shot at her with murderous intent, wounding her in the right side. Her only daughter now lives with the Pokagon band in Michigan, and well remembers hearing her mother relate the circumstances connected with the tragical affair.

Osh-ki o-gi-maw (young chief), let me tell you some things I have seen in my time at some of our trading posts—even at Mi-shi-nemack-i-nong (Mackinaw Island) where Astor got rich, and we very poor."[2] "Say on," I said. "Well," said he, "nin gi-wab (I have seen) some of our people on the island so diseased with that curse that they would sell au-zhausk (muskrat) skin for a sewing-thimble full of it; a suc-see (deer) skin for a gill of it; au-mick (a beaver) skin for a glass of it; maw-kwa (a bear) skin for a pint of it; mash-ko-de-pi-ji-ki (a buffalo) skin, well tanned, for a quart of it. Do think of it!" I tried to do so, but tired nature, in its weakness, said to my heart, "Go to sleep."

At break of day the old man was up, calling, "Non-nee, Lo-da, Ko-bun-da! No-ki, a-bin-dis nit-a-am (come, get up); we must start." All at once arose, and mother hastily collected the fragments of the previous day's feast for our guests on their way home. Just as the sun kissed the topmost branches of the trees on the surrounding hills, we all stood on the river's shore, and there shaking hands, good-by said, as they stepped into the boat. As I was pushing the craft off the shore into the stream, a strange desire deep down in my heart came welling up, alluring me to give the maid a parting good-by kiss; but through fear I hesitated. Not because of her mother or mine, nor on account of the old man or little boy,—no, not that; for the girls and boys of our people, unlike those of the pale-faced race, are not laughed at and tormented as though it were a crime to fall in love. I said that I hesitated; but it was not on account

---

2. Indian Whisky: The most profitable and the most ruinous trade Mackinaw ever had was in whisky. A well-known recipe among the traders was: "Take two gallons of common whisky, or unrectified spirits, to thirty gallons of water, add red pepper enough to make it fiery, and tobacco enough to make it intoxicating." Its cost was not more than five cents a gallon. Thousands of barrels were sold there every year; the price there generally was fifty cents a quart by the bottle. It is estimated that over half the fish caught and fur sold there for thirty years was paid for by the above compound, and that more than half of the annuities the Indians received from the United States was expended to purchase it. The most wealthy and respectable traders on the island were not ashamed to deal in it. Think of it!

A short time ago I stayed all night at the old Astor house on the island, which now is run for a hotel. The old Astor books are still kept there as relics of early days.

In the books of 1817 and 1818 and so on, I found the invoice for whisky exceeded that of all other goods. The handwriting is the plainest I ever saw.

As I was examining them, I thought in my heart, if these books are ever required in the supreme court of Heaven as evidence against the white man for dealing out "ish-kot-e-waw-bo" to the red man, no experts will be necessary to read them.

of any humankind. But there stood that jealous deer, watching every move I made. Say, was it wrong for me to wish that he was dead?

Just then like some anxious dog to go, that starts before his master's team, he started off before the boat, bounding up the stream along the shore. Quickly I seized Lonidaw's hand, and holding it aloft, our lips half-way in mutual concert met. No word we said; our hearts endeared, beat time to the tune of youthful love no language can express. Unlike the savage practise of the whites, our little band no sneering laugh passed round. Pushing the boat from off the shore, I said, "Me-no tchi-ki (Good-by) until we meet again." I hoped to see her shed a parting tear, but she simply waved her hand and smiled "me-no tchi-ki."

I watched the boat, with its living jewel crowned, sweep round the river's bend, while every now and then, through bush and brake, I faintly glimpsed the snow-white deer, in contrast with the green, bounding along the shore. Just as they were out of sight, Maw-kaw came rushing down the terrace of the stream, whining and frisking about as if we had been gone a month or more, stealing kisses every now and then, saying by every act and look, "Let us rejoice that they are gone."

On the following day, my old-time friend, Bertrand, came after us according to promise, at the third full moon, to take us home. As we were packing our goods into his boat, I noticed a basket of curious make, with wild rice trimmed, as if growing in the water. In seating myself in the boat to steer, I asked, "What in the world is that for?" He replied, "Sime, me guess me by me vill show you wid him how me used to catch um duck alive!" In passing down the Sebe we came to a wild-rice cove, in which some wild ducks were feeding. Here the old man dropped his oars, saying, "Now, Sime, me by me vill catch a pair of them ducks by their feet alive." So saying, he put the basket over his head, and jumped into the stream, the water just covering his shoulders. Slowly he walked in the water toward the ducks; the box trimmed with rice straw appeared to be floating toward the flock, soon moving among them. They appeared to realize no fear of danger from the floating craft. Anxiously my mother and I watched, as he moved among them. Soon I saw one duck sink like lead out of sight; then another disappeared, leaving scarcely a sparkle where they sank. Slowly the rice craft came floating back, until it reached the boat. The old man then handed us the box, which we placed in the boat, with a pair of the beautiful ducks safely secured.

After reaching home, in a few days reluctantly I returned to school. While there, during the following fall and winter time, my heart almost continually whispered, "How strange it seems!" I left the white man's school, to dwell a while in solitude, close to "ki-ji-o daw" (the great heart) of nature, and read her soul-inspiring books. It was not in my thoughts to find in such a wild retreat a lovely maiden of our race; and to find one anywhere who could arouse such tender love within my breast, had never been suggested to my mind, in sleep or awake. Most faithfully I tried to convince myself that my love was not of Heaven born, as we are taught, from sire to son, that to be pure its origin must be divine. But I feared in my heart that it was earthly, that it was transient, and never could last. I struggled on and on to free myself from its tightening coils; but like the panther in a snare held fast, I struggled all in vain. The more I strove, the closer clung her image to my heart; until, tired of war, at length I yielded to the charm; convinced such sacred love and fond desire *must be* of origin divine.[3] When springtime came, and the deep snows began to melt away, I started for the land of the Ottawas to find the dear romantic maid.

Four days northward I held my course alone, along an ancient trail, through tangled cedar swamps, and over hills through dense "jin-gwak" (pine) and "ka-gag-i-wanj-kig" (hemlock woods), where winter's snows still lay deep upon the ground. Each night my bed was moss and evergreen boughs, such as I could gather from the wilds about me. Undisturbed, save by the distant howl of wolves and hooting owls close by, I passed the nights in fondest dreams, in company with the one whose loving image was deeply impressed upon "nin-o-daw" (my heart). Arriving near where I supposed Loni-daw lived, I met two boys with bows and arrows armed, each carrying a string of "o-me-me-og"

---

3. I have often wondered why Christian people should still cling to the idolatrous practise of symbolizing love affairs with Cupid and his bow shooting darts of love. It certainly has a tendency to demoralize its sacred and divine origin. I am fully pursuaded it originated from an ancient people whose ideal of true love was far in the background, as compared with the American Indians.

Much has been said and written, by white men, of our people marrying for so many moons. It has been published to the world, through the influence of white traders, who in times past have come among us, marrying Indian girls so as to be in closer touch with our people, to aid them in buying and selling; and after forsaking them, and their *own* children, to return again to their people, branding us with that accursed lie to shield their own disgrace.

The fact has never been denied that our people, prior to the discovery of America, had no venereal diseases among them.

The social gift of God, for the propagation of the human family, was never bought and sold by our people; no, nor such a thing thought of, until introduced by civilization.

(wild pigeons) and "au-saw-naw-gog" (squirrels) around their shoulders tied. After looking their game over and asking them many questions which I thought might please them to impart, I finally inquired if either of them knew where an old Indian lived by the name of Kaw-be-naw. One of them, a white boy, promptly replied, "I guess me by we do. He's dat boy's oldest granddad." I then asked the other boy, who was Indian, where his granddad lived. The little redskin walked inquiringly about, looking me carefully over, and finally said, "Kaw-in ne-ge-wob how-yea o-gaw-she-maw ne-be-nong?" (Did I not see you and your mother way down the river last summer?) "Are you Non-nee on-son (little Nonnee)?" I asked. With a pleasant smile he answered, "Me guess me by me be." I remarked, "I did not know you with that red blanket on." "Guess me by me neber not know you dressed like um big Injun." I then shook hands with the little fellow, telling him I was indeed glad to see him, then asked, "Is this Sketer, the white boy that taught you to talk like smokemon?" "Me guess me by he be; and me learn him to talk like Injun." I then shook hands with the boy professor, telling him I had heard him spoken of as a good English teacher. Then turning to Nonnee, I said, "You have not told me yet where I can find your granddad." He replied in a don't-care manner, "O, down dat trail me by little way." I walked on in the direction he pointed. I had gone but a few steps when I was halted by hearing, "Pogon, Pogon! Hold on, stop! me want to talk more wid you." He then came to me on the run, saying, "Me by you would like to see um Loda? We are going down to her wigwam, to let her see um pigeon and squirrel." He then said, "Say, Loda talk much about you, she do—good many times. Come," he said, taking me by the hand, "go down there wid us; then me by we go wid *you* and see granddad. I tell you we will have lots and lots of fun. Say, Loda has been and got au-ni-mouns au-ni-moosh (a puppy dog) named Zo-wän; sure as you lib, she has. And say, her deer am just as mad as him can be." "Where did she get him?" I asked. "She got 'im last fall, she did; but no bring home until de deer's horns fall off. Me tells you, Pogon, you otter see de deer go for dat dog. He bite 'im de deer's nose all de time all to pieces, and make 'im bleed and blat like sixty." "Well," I said, "does that please Loda?" "Me don't know; me by not," he said, "for she put her arms about his neck, and pat 'im on o-daw-me-con (the jaw), and say, 'Me-no waw-mawsh-kay-she (Do be good deer); me by Pogon come bine by, and if you be bad to him, me will sell you to smokemon showman.' Come, do go down and see um fight." While

Nonnee was urging me to go to see the fun, Sketer would chime in every now and then, with a laughing grin, "Come, go down wid us and see um fight."

I finally gave consent; and as we walked along, I could plainly see that the boys were in fear that I might give up going with them, for they were continually assuring me that it was but a little ways farther on. I was indeed glad they did not know that I had crossed the country a hundred miles or more, on foot and alone, through ice and snow, to reach the very place they were so fearful I might not go to, to see the fun. I said, "Nonnee, I think it very strange that Loda should keep a puppy dog to bite and torment her deer." He stood still, looking me square in the face, showing by his looks that he was determined to defend her, and said, "Me tells you, Pogon, her deer got orful bad, him did. Last fall Loda make nice willow cage, and put in him nesh-kwaw-notch mis-kwa pe-nay-shen-og (a pair of real pretty red birds) which I and Sketer give her, and dat deer got so mad, him did, him rare up above de door, pawed de cage down, and grind him wid his horns all to pieces, and kill um bof birds, him did! Tink of dat! Loda me guess do right she do."

We reached the wigwam. It was snugly built with poles and logs and painted bluish-white with clay. As I walked up to the wigwam, the boys, all excited, rushed in front of me opening wide the door, and exclaiming, "Wab-saw-naw-gog wab-o-me-me-og!" (See the squirrels and the pigeons!) Nonnee then said, "Loda! O Loda! we find Pogon back in the woods, and make him come down here wid us to see the fun with the puppy dog and the deer." There I stood, just outside the door, with my heart fluttering like a wounded bird; and she just inside, so pale I doubted if it were her. I finally stammered out, "Boo-zhoo-nic-con;" retiringly, she repeated back the greeting which I gave, then said, "Pin-di-gayn" (come in). In I walked, and asked, while shaking hands, "Pin-dig-ke o-gaw-she-maw?" (Is your mother in?) She replied, "Kaw-win (no), she is in is-kí-gán-is-a-gán ji-wa-gán-is-i-gán (the sugar-camp making maple molasses), but will soon be ke-win (home)." The walls within the room were lined with mats of different make and size with colors gay, while from the ceiling hung baskets great and small of curious make, adorned with artificial leaves and flowers, inwrought with shreds of bark and various-colored quills. In one corner of the room bundles of rushes, sweetgrass, and flags were snugly stored away, richly perfuming all within the room. In the meantime, as I surveyed the curious place, the boys had overhauled the puppy dog,—a great big fellow nearly grown,—and thrust him into my arms. Holding him there, I said, "Lonidaw, where is waw-mawsh-kay-she?" Smiling, she replied, "Aus-kwe-yong-wigwam (Behind the house); aw-yaw o-da au-ko-zee (he is sick at heart)." Sketer now spoke out, "Him ant sick, but mad about this puppy dog bein' here—dat's what ales de deer." Nonnee now stepped forward, pulling the dog out of my arms, at the same time addressing Loda, saying, "Come, let's take him out where de deer be, and let Pogon see the darndest fight him eber seed." Both boys continued to clamor, urging her to let them fight, until she stepped outside the door, and called out, "Non-nee, Non-nee, pes-saw-gon (come out here)." The boy went out. She talked with him there quietly for some time; I never knew what she said. He came back into the house, whispered to Sketer, when both picked up their bows and arrows, together with their game, and started out. On his way, Nonnee said, "O Loda, granddad wants you to fetch him some si-wit-a-gan (salt) when you come over." Then turning to me he said, "Me guess me by me tell granddad you be here, and he will come right ober and see you. He talks lots about you, he does." I said, "My boy, you tell your granddad that I will come over and see him; for if he starts, we may miss each other on the way, and not see each other at all."

The darling of my heart and I were now left alone. I knew it was a golden chance, and summoning all my courage, I said, "Lonidaw, my heart has mourned to meet with you ever since we parted at the river's side last summertime. I have sought you for four days, through rain and shine, through ice and snow, not only to tell you that I love you, but also to say that I am anxious you shall be nin wa-wid-i-ged ikwe (my bride)." Pale and surprised, the maiden looked at me, but not a word she said. And going on, I said, "Lonidaw, I am no ga-gi-e-win do-dam-o-win[4] (ogler), but boldly speak my honest heart's desire. If you can not now consent, tell me, fair girl, if there is room for hope." Statue-like she stood, and for a time as dumb. At length, most pathetically, she said, "You call me gi-ga-kwe (girl), and well you may, for so I am; but ni-aw (alas) sir, nin-gaw (my mother) says, "Gi-os-se au-nishi-naw-be (A hunted race) like ours should kaw-win wi-wi-ma (never wed)." I replied, "Dear one, I have lived for years with the pale-

---

4. A timid lover who runs about outside the wigwam of o-se-wan mit-taw-win (his sweetheart) trying to act out his love, instead of telling it to her, in order to influence her to become his wife.

faced race; they have always used me well." "Yes," she said, "I learn that you have, and you can talk well with them in their o-da-naw (tongue), and read their books, but I am but pa-gwag ab-i-not ji mit-tig (a wild child of the woods), wild as ben-ish ig (the birds) that gather round to hear nin-na-gam na-gam-on (me sing the songs) they chant, as I pass along ki mit-i-gwa-ki mi-kan-og (our woodland trails). I can only speak well nin-gaw o-da-naw (my mother tongue). With my mother and our people, nin min-wen-dam (I am happy); but should we wed, I fear you soon would tire of my native woodland ways, and crush this childish o-daw nin (heart of mine)." "No, no, not so," I said. "I would forsake the white man's land, and live the life that you have led. Your people should be my people, and we would live as our fathers lived, before the white man came among us. Yes, I am willing, my dear girl, for your sake, to surrender all the aspirations that ever were mine to become learned and great, that I might enjoy the heaven-born love that I have for thee, and thee alone." Thus did I plead my cause to gain her native heart. Her mother came at last, surprised to find me there. Each hand of mine in hers she grasped, and with a twofold shake, a hearty "Boo-zhoo-nic-con" she said, inquiring all about my mother's health, and what had brought me there. No answer did I give. At length the daughter, weeping, told how I had been pleading for her heart and hand. As I listened to her plaintive voice, and gazed upon her childlike face of innocence, tears came trickling down my cheeks, and down her mother's, too. Silence for a while reigned supreme within the room, unbroken by our sighs alone. At length sympathy gave way to reason's sway, and we three talked on and on, of joining "o-daw a-chi o-nind-ji-ma" (heart and hand), until the morning dawned, and then the mother said, "Nin e-taw mi-gi-we (I only give consent) because no-ko-miss (your grandmother), when I was left nin ma-mi-maw-is nin-gi-win (an orphan at my birth), took care of me, and brought me up with di-ben-dan (your own dear mother), who was on-da-dis gi-gig tchi-baw (born the day before). Yes, it is because ki-ja nin a-bin-og-i-win (your mother and I in infancy) nursed and fondled the same to-tosh (breast) together, and in childhood shared each other's joys and fears together. And in kish-kin-jig (your face) I trace the pleasing lines your mother and her mother always wore. Hence, I give consent, for I owe to your family line a deep debt of gratitude no other gift can fully pay. But, Si-maw, you must not bo-nem-dam ki-tchi man-i-to (forget that the Great Spirit) will watch your treatment of my only child, who was in sorrowing exile born. Ae, mi-kwen-dam (Yes, remember), too, ki mish-ke-si-kan (his eyes) are kesus ke-zhe-gut (the sun by day) and te-bi-ke-sus au-nong-wog te-bi-cut (the moon and stars by night); hence remember this—kaw-win ke-taw gawsh-to-se tchi gaw ke-taw-wod me-no Mau-ni-to! (You can not hide yourself, nor your acts, from God!)"

Those sacred words from a true mother's lips sank deep into my youthful heart. Never did two turtle-doves, just before their nesting time, more tenderly press each other's bills, than did we each other's lips that morning dawn to seal our marriage vow.

VI

A t sunrise, as we were sitting on a rug, of sweetgrass and rushes made, Lonïdaw sitting close beside me, with "Zowän" (the dog) in front, "nin-gaw" (her mother) opened wide the door to let the sunlight in. There, just outside, facing us, stood the sacred deer; but he was a mere skeleton of his former self. Motionless he seemed to stand, with head drooped low and hair upturned, with wounded nose and frothing mouth, with lolling tongue and wilted ears, with sunken eyes and antlers gone,—there he stood the very personification of "ga-we-win" (jealousy).[1]

Springing to my feet in haste, I said, "Is that your deer, or o-tchi-bai (his ghost)." "Do not leave me," she said, "but let us walk out in front of him on-ind-ji-ma on-ind-ji-ma (hand in hand), for he must learn to control tchi-gaw-e o-daw (that jealous heart of his); if not, when kin-esh-kan (his antlers) again are grown, he may nish-iwe win e-taw-waw (kill us both)." So we joined hands, and with Zowän walking between us, we boldly marched out, and stood in front of him! He shook his head, turned about, stepped a few feet away, there a moment stood, then turned around, facing us with the most forlorn look I ever beheld; "the green-eyed monster" trembled in despair, and walked sullenly away, as if he hated "kaw-ki-naw ke-kog" (all things) and himself. He never after could be found—though hunters oft, in after years, would tell how they had bent "o-mit-ig-wab" (their bow) to shoot a deer of red, when lo! their hands were stayed; and to their great surprise Lonidaw's sacred deer of white before them for a moment stood, then vanished out of sight!

After eating our simple morning meal of "mand-a-min" (corn-cakes) in "gi-wa-ga-mis-i-gan" (maple syrup) dipped, and pudding of "man-o-min" (wild rice) and "aj-a-we-min" (beechnuts) made, I proposed to Loda to go with me and visit Uncle Kaw-be-naw. After getting "maw-kok-on-son" (a small bark box) with salt therein for the old man, we started, she leading the way through dark "ka-gag-i-wang" (hemlock) and "aj-a-we-min mit-tig" (beech woods). As we were passing quietly

---

1. With our people, "she-gog" (the skunk) represents jealousy, from the fact that its odor is not only awfully offensive to other creatures, but frequently when tormented, it suffers death from its own stink.

along, I said, "Loda, as I lay concealed among the tall ferns by mi-kaw-naw (the trail) side near ki-nib-i-win (your camp) last summer-time, you passed along that way, chattering au-saw-nog-gog (the squirrels') sneezing, scolding bark. While you were yet scarce out of sight, followed by your deer, squirrels red, black, and gray came following on your track, and flocked about the trail where you had passed along. Then I thought it strange indeed; but when Kaw-be-naw came after you, he told me how you could gather, by your alluring call, mona-to-awk (wild beasts) and bi-nes-sig (fowls); then I knew how came so many squirrels there. I have noticed, as we have passed along, many flocks of o-me-me-og (wild pigeons) passing and repassing high in air; come, now, please do show nin kin-gash-ku-wis-i-win (me your power) in calling these birds together." With pensive look and downcast eyes, modestly she replied, "Simaw, to please you I will try."

So saying, she stepped aside, and found a bare spot of ground in an opening where "ke-sus" (the sun) had melted "sag-i-po" (the snow) away. Here she raked off the leaves, exposing "a-ki" (the ground) to view, and sprinkled salt thereon; then with evergreen branches she trimmed my clothes and hers, and we both sat down on "mit-ig" (a log). She then said, "Min-o-tam, pe-naw, pe-naw" (Keep still and listen). She then commenced a lively chattering, reminding me somewhat of several "ki-tchi pa-ka-ak-weg" (old hens) all calling their broods at the same time, to partake of their morning meal; but her notes were longer, more varied, and musical. One pigeon after another dropped on the bare spot of "a-ki" (earth), until they piled on top of each other like starving "amog" (bees) upon a piece of "amo-si-sib'-a-kwat" (honeycomb), all chattering in harmony with her musical voice, creating a novel concert, somewhat like that of unnumbered "o-ma-ka-kig" (frogs) in springtime, in early morning.

Still they continued to increase in numbers, pouring in from all directions, filling every bush and tree, and alighting on the ground. Looking up, I saw high above the trees, multitudes falling like meteors from heaven with sky-rocket sound to the earth, until acres were blue with them. At some signal given by the watch-sentinels with a sharp clap of "nin-gwi-gan-og" (the wings), the vast numbers would rise with the roar of "an-a-mi-ke" (thunder) and sweep in circles around us, hiding the sun from view, and continually increasing in numbers. Then with her musical chattering, she would call them back, when they would sweep down like an infant cyclone, covering the ground and trees all about us, frequently lighting on our heads and shoulders. It was a most endearing sight to behold these beautiful flowers of the animal creation in their native state close by, with their brilliant coloring of gold and royal purple intermixed, outrivaling the beauty of the rainbow. I caught a pair of these wonderful birds, but Lonidaw persuaded me to let them go by telling me that if I should do them harm she might lose her power to charm. Disrobing ourselves of the evergreen branches, and stepping out among them, the vast body rose at once, causing the earth to tremble as if shaken by "ni-ning-a-kami-gis-ka-a-ki" (an earthquake).

After they had gone, I could think of nothing but a calm after a great storm. Finally I broke the silence by saying, "Loda, do tell me how your chattering so allures those birds." She replied, "Not far north of here, for miles and miles the trees are spotted with their nests.[2] For some cause, while hatching and rearing their young they are frantic for salt, and when one of them finds a salt spring, or salty ground, they spread the good news by chanting as I did; and this is what they shout, 'Se-taw-kin, se-taw-kin, au-zhon-daw, au-zhon-daw' (Salt, salt, salt is here)! The cry is passed along the line, and all that hear the pleasing call rush to the scene like warriors to battle." We now passed on, until we reached the old man's hut. It was a round stockade, about sixteen feet across the base and twelve feet high; the posts leaned inward, leaving "paw-kwe-ne" (a smoke-hole) at the top. A monster dog, with long, black hair lay stretched out on his side before the door. A young "wau-goosh" (fox) was playing about him. On hearing us, the dog got up and came toward us. Loda greeted him, "Boo-zhoo." He answered back, "Bow-wow-wow," in heavy bass, and tried to kiss her face; but pushing

---

2. I have visited many wild pigeons' nesting grounds in the early days in Indiana, Wisconsin, and Michigan, that extended fifteen or twenty miles, covering thousands of acres, where nearly every tree was spotted with their nests. I have known these birds in Michigan to commence nesting where the ground under them was covered with two feet of snow. They use from fifty to one hundred sticks in building a nest, which they sometimes carry several miles. I have known them to fly over one hundred miles to procure food. Beech mast is their favorite food when nesting; but if necessary, will feed on any kind of nut they can swallow, and seeds and berries as well. It was proverbial among our fathers that if God could have created a more beautiful bird than the wild pigeon, he certainly never had done so. In the *Chautauquan* magazine of November, 1895, there is an interesting article by the chief on the wild pigeons of North America, which ought to be read by all lovers of the bird creation who would like a better knowledge of these wonderful birds.

him away, she said, "Sit up, Ma-quaw." He sat up on his haunches like a bear, after which he was named. She then said, "This is Chief Pokagon; give him your hand." Reaching out "waw-na-sia" (his paw), I gave it a hearty shake. She then said to him, "Mauch-on (Go away) and lie down." He obeyed. As we stepped before the open door, the old man was busy bow- and arrow-making. We greeted him, "Boo-zhoo-nic-con." He sprang to the door, repeating back our greeting, and grasping Lonidaw's right hand and my left in his, he led us kindly into his hut and set us down on robes of beaver made, assuring us he was heart-glad we had come, and that he had remained at home because Non-nee had told him that Pokagon was coming to see him, and that he had prepared "we-kau-de-win-on-son" (a small barbecue).

The room was lined with skins of various kinds, and so arranged that they almost seemed alive,—me-she-be-she (the panther) crouching here as if to pounce upon "wa mawsh-ka-she" (the deer), and "pe-zhen" (the lynx) lay low as if to spring upon "maw-boos" (the rabbit) passing by, while "she-go-se," "shaw-guay-she," and "wau-goosh" (the weasel, mink, and fox), with "au-saw-naw-gog" (the squirrels) played their cunning part. A blazing fire was in the center of the room. The old man began at once telling about my father's moral courage in not allowing "fire-water" to to be bought or sold among his band, and as he talked, he was engaged in sharpening some sticks at both ends, upon one end of which, when finished, he stuck dressed pigeons, sticking the opposite ends into the ground, leaning them inward toward "ish-ko-te" (the fire). While broiling there, he would sprinkle them with salt, turning the sticks every now and then, in order to cook them evenly and well. Their sweet odor sharpened my appetite to the boiling-point. When all were nicely browned, he said, "Take your pick and help kin-a-waw-win (yourselves)." We did so, eating with our hands like "kek-kek-og" (hawks) "osh-kan-gin" (with their claws), throwing the bones, when picked, into the fire. When I had supposed the meal was eaten, the old man raked from the embers several birds wrapped in large, wet leaves, undressed and unpicked, saying, "Me-no o-me-me-og (Good pigeons) cook all day." I now began to realize that the old man was putting on style, and had prepared a second course.

I had never seen birds cooked in that style before; but as Loda stripped off the feathers from one, and commenced eating it with a relish, I did likewise, finding it well done, and was fully satisfied that I had never before eaten meat more pleasing to the taste. Just then

Nonnee and Sketer came to the door, whistling and calling, "Maw-kaw, Maw-kaw." The old dog rushed to the door, but no sooner had he stepped outside than he gave a whining yelp and backward came into the house, shaking his head, snuffing and bleeding at the nose, while at the same time some dark object rolled into the fire, scattering embers all about. To our surprise "mi-shi mi-ki-nock" (a big snapping-turtle), with snake-like head protruding from his shell, came waddling toward us, scattering sparks and ashes as he came! The old man seized the strange intruder and hurled him out of the door, saying, "You young maw-chi-og (rascal), what do you mean?" then turning to Sketer, said, "You little wa-be-en-ami-as-sig (white heathen, you), get right away from here; you are bound to ruin Non-nee." The boy retorted back, "Me done nofin. Nonnee called the dog out, he did, to show 'im mi-ki-nock, and him went to smell 'im, and him snap his nose, him did!" Then facing Nonnee, the old man said, "Ki pan-gi-she manito (You little imp), come into the wigwam." With drooping head, the boy came in as though he expected to be whipped; but when he saw the old man had been eating, he said, "Hold on nim-ish-o-mis (granddad), don't eat all the o-me-me-og up; me am most starved to death." The old man quietly taking the boy by the shoulders, said, "Mi-no-ak (keep still); did you know Chief Pokagon is here?" The boy, turning to me, said, "Hello, Po-gon, how de do?" The old man now from the embers raked more steaming birds. As they rolled out on the hearth, the boy grabbed one, shook off the leaves, clawed off the feathers, eating like a hungry cat. While stripping the feathers off the second bird, he said, "Well, Loda, has au-ni-mouns, au-ni-moosh, and wa-maw-kav-she had any more fights? Me suppose you and Pogon had lots of fun seein' um fight, after you got me and Sketer away. Me don't care anyway, but think you was just as mean as you *could* be." Upbraiding him, the old man said, "Nonnee kawin nin gi-git (don't you speak) another word. Wau-be-que-we-zayns (That white boy) is learning you to be just as impudent and mau-chi-ish (mean) as you can be." Loda, apparently sorry for the little lad, kindly asked: "Nonnee, tamo-ka ai-aw kin (where have you been)?" He replied, "O, down to ga-gai-gan (the lake) to see um play moccasin. Lots and lots of white folks come too; me guess me by to sell um Injun ish-kot-e-wa-bo (whisky)."

After the feast, the old man was ready to visit. He had no dishes to wash, or kettles to clean. As he lay on his side, reclined on one arm, he began to recount all about the pleasant time he had while at our wigwam fort last summer-time, having a most hearty laugh over Nonnee's deer ride and the bees near the river's shore. He was still, however, mourning over the curse of rum that was being brought among his people; and Loda, I could plainly see, was in deep sympathy with him. He charged her in the name of the Great Spirit never to have anything to do with "osh-ki-naw-we" (a young man) who did not hate the hellish stuff with a deadly hate. Finally he asked me how I felt toward "gotam-igos mautchi" (the frightful curse). I declared most emphatically that I "hated it with a *deadly* hate."

Leaving the old man's hut, Nonnee stood just outside, and picking up the turtle, said, "Here, Loda, see how heavy he be." She replied, "O, ne-que-we-sayns (my boy), do take that poor creature back, and put it in the lake again!" "Why," he said, "Loda, do you know 'im? Have you seen 'im before? Sketer says, every full moon you go down to sa-gia-gan and call upon the shore flock after flock of them snapping-turtles, and that you talk wid 'em and feel their teef wid your fingers, and that they will not bite, but laugh at you. Here," said he, "feel of dis one's teef." As if provoked, she said, "Non-nee, pen-sen-do do-we-shin (listen to me); I once called you ne-ma-ma-gwan (my butterfly), but now, like Sketer, you are getting to be paw-big (a flea). Why can't you be me-no (good), and do as uncle tells you, and keep away from Sketer?" As we started on, the old man quietly said, "Loda, min-o-naw-wea ta-ko-ki-win aw-mi-kan (please step this way)."

She did so. I overheard him say, "Dib-ad-jim o-gin tchi (Tell your mother that Ash-taw will be here) wa-sing-wan (this spring) tchi ki-di-no-amage-o on-ge tchi-gin-jen-dam ish-kot-e-waw bo (to teach the Indian children to hate whisky)."[3]

---

3. Afterward I learned that "Ash-taw" was a woman among the Ottawas renowned as a temperance worker. Her strong hold was to give object-lessons. She traveled from place to place, and wherever she found a few families in a neighborhood, she called the children together to hold a little "powwow" of their own. She always managed to keep on hand a stock of snakes' eggs. She would hold her meetings at such times as some of the egg litters were about to hatch. She stained them a beautiful red color, placing them on green moss in "wig-was-si ma-kak-ogons (small, white birch-bark boxes)' so as to have them appear to the children as charming as possible. After the children were assembled, she called them about her; then opened the boxes one by one in their presence; and when their admiration was sufficiently excited so they all began to inquire what kind of eggs they were, she would make reply, "These are ish-kot-e-waw bo wän-än-ug (whisky eggs);" then she would add, "Would you like to take some of them?" She would then carefully put into each extended hand some of the charming-colored little eggs.

On our return, Lonidaw related how the old man had lost several sons through the use of strong drink, and how some of his daughters and granddaughters were abused by drunken husbands who had made him untold trouble.

As we passed the place on our way home, where "o-me-me-og" in multitudes together she had called that day, I asked how and when she first learned "o-daw-naw-naw" (the language) of beasts and birds. Silently a while she walked along; then answering, said, "You ask me for the sacred gimo-disiwin (secret) of nin-o-daw (my heart), which never yet has been told; but to you alone it shall be given, in perfect trust not to be revealed. First nin gash-kiton mi-kwen-dass (I can remember) in early girlhood, is of being delighted with nag-a-mon (the songs) of birds; yet I knew not what caused the pleasing sound. When older grown, I stole away from nin-gaw (my mother) to find the source from whence it came. While watching in some hazel brush, one bright morning in spring, au-pe-tchi (a robin) came, and lighted just above me, pouring forth its joyful song of praise, so close that I could plainly see every motion of win o-kog (its bill) and swelling gon-ga-gan (throat). Unconsciously I too began to sing its warbling na-ga-mon (song), and in after years, when mating birds each other wooed, I sang with them their soft and tender strains of sa-gia-we-win (love); when awakened by alarm, I joined with them in their shrill and startling cries; when assailed by birds of prey, I joined them in their shout of defiance; when their nests were robbed, I joined them in their bitter moans; when their young abandoned their nests and flew away, I joined them in their plaintive chirps to call them back; when their companions were lost, I sang with them the funereal dirge. And so it was I learned and loved to mourn, and to rejoice with them, and grew in sympathy with all the tenants of the woods."

On receiving them, childlike they would feel of the little beauties with the tips of their fingers, when to their great surprise, the frail egg shells would crumble away, and from each come forth a little snake squirming and wriggling in their hands. Then with a shriek of horror they would let the young reptiles drop, and scatter like leaves in a whirlwind. The cruel joke impressed their youthful minds with such a loathsome hate against ish-kot-e-waw-bo that their very souls ever after would revolt at the sight, smell, or even thought of the deceptive curse.

This shrewd woman would then make an application of the strong object-lesson, convincing the children that what they had witnessed was but a slight foretaste of the awful reality, and that they who drank, after awhile would be tormented with "mi-chi-gin-e-big" (great big snakes), which they could not escape, or even let go of.

VII

Just before reaching her mother's wigwam, some one called out, "Loda, Loda!" She turned about, exclaiming, "E-nau-bin! E-nau-bin!" (Look! Look!) I did so, and saw approaching a tall, middle-aged man of the Ottawa tribe, dressed in native style, leading a large, gray wolf along the trail toward us. Loda, stepping backward, exclaimed, "Ne-ge-bawn! (My soul!) Kaw-kee, where did you get tchi maw-in-gawn (that wolf)?" "Down by the Se-be," he replied. As I stepped to one side, looking the wild animal over, noticing his drooping head and straightened tail, with sneaky eyes upturned, I was about to speak to the stranger, when he said, "As I passed Kaw-be-naw's back here, he told me young Chief Pokagon, son of old Chief Pokagon, of the Pottawattamie tribe of the south, had just left his lodge for this place." He then asked, "Are you the old og-i-maw (chief's) son?" I replied, "I am." He then asked, "Have you been attending school at Twinsburg, O., with Petoskey and Blackbird, of Traverse Bay?" "I have," I replied. He then said, "I well knew your father, and have frequently heard those two young men speak of you attending the white man's school with them, and have had a great desire to see you. Come, go home with me and stay all night." Turning to Loda, I said, "Had I best go?" "Go, of course," she said, "he is meno aw-nish-naw-by (a good Indian man). He lives in the old Ot-ta-wa council-house." Her answer was sorely disappointing to me, as I had expected she would urge me to stay all night at her mother's. I then said to the stranger, "I will go with you; but do not care to walk near the wolf." Kaw-kee starting on, I followed at a safe distance in the rear. I said, "If that is a wild wolf, I can not understand how you can or dare lead him." "When a boy," he replied, "I went with an old wolf hunter to look after nin das-on-a-gan (his traps); in one we found a large maw-in-gawn (wolf). As we stood looking at the animal, he said, 'Ne-que-we-zayns (my boy), let me show you the nature of maw-in-gawn.' He then cut a gad, as long as I am tall; then taking him by the nape of the neck, he gave him a severe whipping, then tied a rope about his neck, and I led him to his lodge as though he were o-nawm (a dog)." On reaching his wigwam, I saw at a glance that it was an ancient council-house of giant size. Stepping to the door, the stranger said, as he pulled the latchstring, "My people are out in Isk-l-gam-i-sa-gan (the sugar camp); go in and rest while I take care of maw-in-gawn." Slowly I entered, and closed the door.

Silence reigned supreme within the spacious room. Wondering, I stood and gazed; for all about the clay-washed timbered room, as if peering through the walls, hung heads of "mooz," "me-shay-wog," and "waw-mawsh-kay-she" (the moose, the elk, and the deer), with antlers broad; while "maw-quaw," "bi-su," and "es-si-ban" (the bear, the wildcat, and the lynx), with staring eyes all fixed toward the center of the room, where, floating in mid-air with wings extended wide, appeared "mi-gi-si," "kek-kek," and "ko-ko-ko" (the eagle, the osprey, and the owl), watching beneath, where council fires had blazed in former years. Around the sacred altar standards were stuck, on which at half-mast hung old worn-out and tattered hides, on which were painted animals of different kinds, emblems and to-toms of many northern tribes, while from the ceiling swung bunches of "me-daw-win" (corn in the ear), and hammocks large and small, while snowshoes and moccasins hung in pairs on long lines across the room in wedge-shaped rows, graded from infant size up to the full-grown man. It was indeed a novel place, and so reminded me of boyhood days while yet my father lived, I really wished I was a child again. At length Kaw-kee marched into the room, followed by his wife and children nine, in single file, all standing erect as if by military rule. Looking with pride along the line from "ikwe" (wife) to youngest "a-bin-o-gi" (child), he said, "This awosh-ki' ogi'-maw (young chief) is son of old Pokagon, the great Pot-ta-wat-ta-mie chief who once owned She-gog-ong (Chicago), the most loyal and bravest man that ever ruled a tribe." They all gazed at me, as though I was a king of some great nation. I bowed, saying "Boo-zhoo" as royally as I could. All nodded back, repeating in tones suppressed, "Boo-zhoo." He then said, "This is the young chief that Petoskey and Blackbird have talked so much about, who attended the same white man's school where they have been." After the curious eyes of little and big had carefully looked me over, they reclined upon robes that lay scattered about the floor, and all was still. At length I said, "Blackbird, of whom you speak, told me while at school that when he was in the government blacksmith shop at the mission on Grand Traverse Bay, some Indian brought mi-shi au-kick (a monstrous kettle) made of pure copper for him to put a bail in, which tradition said was found in the woods centuries before. Did you ever hear anything about it?" "Yes," he replied, "young chief, I have, and have seen that kettle many times myself. Our tradition is clear, that nearly two hundred and fifty years ago We-me-gen-de-bay, a noted chief of ours, while hunting in the wilderness near where we now are, found mi-shi au-kick (a monstrous kettle) made of pure copper; when found, it was nearly covered with earth, and roots of large trees had grown around and over it. When taken out, it appeared as though it had never been used; there was a round, bright spot in the center of the bottom of it, as though it had been lately made. It was kept for years and years as a sacred relic, hidden in an obscure place unfrequented by man, and was only used on mi-she-we-kaw-de-win ke-zhe-gut-og (for great feast days)." "Where did your people think it came from?" I asked. "Our fathers thought," said he, "that it was made by some deity who presided over au-kee (the country) about here. That kettle is still kept among us, and is now called Man-i-to au-kick (God's kettle), and is used for boiling on-si-ban sho-po-maw (maple sap into sugar) instead of cooking suc-see (deer) or auqua (bear) for feasts. From that relic and many others found by us, we have concluded that this country was once inhabited by a more civilized race than ours."

After disposing of the kettle question, he gave a very interesting history of Petoskey and Blackbird, my Indian school chums, whose tribe and people I had never seen.

In the course of the evening, I was much interested in the following account of Ottawa superstition: "About one year ago," said Kaw-kee, "I had two men employed in cutting cord wood. One day they returned, pale and excited, saying, 'O, Kaw-kee! we cut down a large in-in-a-tig (maple tree), and when we had sawn off the but cut, naw! dash nash-ke! (lo, and behold!) on the end of the log, stained in the wood, was a plain picture of Ki-je Man-i-to (God) before he made au-kee (the world), and we dare not remain in the woods longer, fearing something awful would happen if we did!'

"I a-i-au'-ni (laughed) at them for their foolishness. They tried to get me to go with them and see the strange picture; but as I was sick at the time, and could not go, I persuaded them to go back and cut off a slice from the end of the log, and bring it to me, that I might see the picture for myself. In the course of the day they came back more excited than before. 'Where is the picture?' I asked. 'O, Kaw-kee!' they said, 'we cut off the end of the log as you told us, and as the piece fell picture side down, lo, and behold! on the other side was a plain picture of God *after* he had made the world, and we dare not meddle any farther with it, for we do fear something awful will happen if we do!' On the following day I went into the woods with them. I must admit, as we approached the tree, I felt a sort of reverential awe about my heart. Carefully I picked up the piece sawn from the end of the log, and looked it over first on one side and then the other, being indeed astonished, for on each side Nature, with her own hand, had drawn wonderful pictures."

Getting interested in the wonderful story, I said, "What has become of that piece of wood?" "Here it is," he replied, taking it down from the wall and handing it to me.

I looked it carefully over on both sides. It was indeed a natural curiosity, well calculated to deceive the very elect. On one side appeared the figure of a man, with folded arms, standing in what appeared to be the picture of the segment of a rainbow, with a blanket wrapped about him. This they regarded as a picture of God before he made the world. On the opposite side appeared the same figure with his right arm extended at full length, holding a large ball in his hand, as if in the act of throwing it. This they regarded as a picture of God after he had made the world.

The pictures were caused, in some way, by the growth of the timber; the heart, or red part of the wood, forming the figure, which, surrounded by the sap, or white part of the wood, made the outlines clear. As I looked at one side and then the other, I said in my heart, "Those figures might well deceive a saint." [4]

As much as I was interested in the mysterious pictures, I did not cease to feel Lonidaw's image in my heart, coupled with a strong desire to hear something wonderful said about her, so I inquired how long she and her mother had lived among the Ottawas. He replied, "Ever since Loda was osh-ki a-bin-od-ji (an infant);" then added, "I believe she is the most wonderful girl that ever lived." "In what way?" I asked. "O," said he, "she has such a strange control over the animal creation." He then asked, "Have you seen ne-wau-be maw-mawsh-kay-she (her white deer)?" "I have," I replied. "Well," said he, "I do not suppose there is a young man in all the land of the Ot-ta-was who has heard of that deer who dare visit her. He has such gaw-we-win o-daw (a jealous heart) he will allow no rival entertained by her. I expect to hear at most any time of his killing some bin-is osh-kin-awe (innocent young man), but I do hope it will not be you. Loda does not seem to have any sa-gid-i-win (love) whatever for kwi-wi-sens (the boys). She only seeks communion with the Great Spirit through the animal creation; when

---

4. Chief Pokagon was given in after years the piece of wood referred to, which he still has among his old-time relics.

they see her, or hear her voice, they appear to know her. She claims all living creatures have a language of their own, and that she can talk with them, and I believe she can." As soon as the children heard Loda's name spoken, they all came and stood about their father with open mouths and eyes, showing they were wonderfully interested to hear some story about Loda.

One of the smaller children, climbing into his lap, said, "Di-bad-jim ke ge-ga Lo-da a-chi an-deck-og." (Tell him about Loda and the crows.) He commenced, saying: "When Loda was about five years old, as I was passing through the woods near where her mother lives, I heard a great tumult among the crows, intermixed with plaintive cries of smaller birds. I walked quietly to the place where they were coming together in great numbers. I had heard such tumults many times before, and never had failed to find that they were persecuting some straggling ko-ko-ko (owl) caught out napping after sunrise. Of course, Pokagon," said he, "you have many times witnessed the same. Men often have their imaginary tchi-ba-i (ghosts) that most cruelly haunt them at night, but the innocent birds of the forests have their real ghosts in the ko-ko-kog (owls), who steal upon them with their great glaring eyes in the darkness, tearing them asunder with their murderous claws. Hence, no wonder when they are caught out in daylight, and can scarcely see, that war is declared against them, that only closes with the closing day. Now to my story. At the time referred to I crept near the spot where I believed ko-ko-ko was located, as indicated by the movements of the birds, and stood still behind the roots of a large newly upturned tree, and peering through a hole therein, I saw a pair of large eyes staring at the crows as they made their gyrations and divings, uttering their war-whoops for battle.

"I could hear the hiss and bass grunt of the owl as the crows flapped their wings against her, but could not see a crow enter the spice-wood brush from whence the sound came. I bent my bow to its fullest tension, determined to center the owl's head between the eyes. Just as I let the arrow fly, a little girl sprang like a squirrel from out the bush in plain sight. The arrow just missed her head. My heart so fluttered that I could scarcely see. For there within twenty feet of me, all unconscious of danger, stood little Loda, trimmed in ferns and flowers, hopping and laughing, 'haw, haw, haw;' an dek (the crows) flew up into the trees, laughing back 'haw, haw, haw,' seeming to enjoy the joke with her. As she wandered out of sight laughing her 'haw, haw, haw' in concert with the crows, I could follow her course wherever she went by the noise and movements of the birds above her through the trees. I went at once to her mother's wigwam, so as to be present when the little girl came home, as I was anxious to know what kind of a story she would tell her when she returned. I asked her mother, 'Where is Loda?' She did not even know she was absent. In a few minutes she came in bare-footed, wearing a brown dress, with a wreath of trailing arbutus about her head and lone berries strung about her neck. Her mother said, 'Where have you been, Loda?' Very quietly she answered, 'Out in the woods.' 'What doing?' she asked. 'O,' she replied, 'playing haw, haw with pe-nay-shen-og (the birds).' Her mother asked her many questions about the play, but she would tell no more. At length I said, 'Loda, my little pet, I was in mit i gog (the woods) and saw you playing ko-ko-ko gi-gi an deck (owl with the crows). I saw your eyes in a spice-wood brush, and mistook them for the eyes of an owl. Had you delayed one eye-wink of time in jumping from out the bush my pik-wak (arrow) would have pierced you through between the eyes.' While talking to her she stood in one corner of the room watching her toes as she wiggled them about. She finally looked up shyly from under o-maw-mawn (her eye-brows), mischievously saying, 'I guess me by it was some other quay-sayns on-son (little girl) you saw,' and would say no more." I then asked Kaw-kee what kind of boys Nonnee and Sketer were. "Well," said he, "Nonne would be a pretty good boy if he could keep away from Sketer, who is chuck full of little cruel tricks; but Nonnee thinks him awful cunning." Here a little boy spoke up, "Nos (Pa), tell 'im about the deer-mice." The whole family now began to laugh. "Well," said Kaw-kee, "a few days ago the two boys came here. Sketer had a box under his arm. He told our children he had in it some deer-mice that he had taught to turn somersaults in the air. Of course the children were anxious to see the show. The box was opened, and out sprang the deer-mice, bounding among the children all about the room, and turning over and over at every bound, just as Sketer said they would do.[5] At first I really thought the boys had trained them to perform in the manner they did. Finally

---

5. "Wawa-bigon odji" (the deer-mouse) is outdone by no other animal in laying up its winter store. Its favorite food is beech-nuts. It will lay up in some safe log or hollow tree from four to eight quarts, which they shell in the most careful manner. The Indians easily find their stores when the snow is on the ground, by the refuse on the snow. In like manner they locate bee-trees, both of which in the early days was a source of important revenue for them.

I caught one, and found its tail had just been cut off. I then saw the trick at a glance; they had just caught the mice and cut their tails off as they were taken from the box, and when they undertook to leap, as is natural for them in traveling, they were thrown out of balance, turning over several times before they struck the floor. I had to laugh, still was provoked to have my children witness such cruel sport, hence I told the boys to get out right away, and not play with my children any more."

It was nearly midnight before I went to my hammock, still I could not sleep. For the past twenty-four hours I had been under great excitement; had contracted and sealed the marriage vow; had witnessed the jealous, sacred deer, in his discouragement, abandon the home of his mistress on my account; in astonishment had seen the whirlwind of wild pigeons assemble at the magic call of Lonidaw; had partaken of the strange feast at the lodge of Kaw-be-naw; had listened with great interest to the stories of Kaw-kee, and his strange history of Lonidaw; her seeming lack of all love for the opposite sex; all of which, like a merry-go-round, continued to revolve through my mind.

Near break of day I lost myself in sleep, dreaming I went forth to hunt for deer. The snow lay deep upon the ground. With "a-gin-og" (snow-shoes) I traveled on and on, through forests dark and drear, but not a track could anywhere be found. As the sun was sinking low, a deer bounding before me came. I pierced him with an arrow through, and while yet the snow his life's blood drank, he changed from red to white; when lo! Lonidaw's sacred deer of white before me dying lay. Loud he groaned, "Loda! Loda! Loda!" and sprang into the air, transformed into a bird of giant size, bearing me away above the trees and valleys deep and broad, and mountains high, while at every motion of his wings I felt that I must surely fall; till tired at length of holding on, headlong I fell, awakening with a scream. So real it seemed, I could not believe that it was all a dream.

Late in the morning I called to see my promised bride. Her face was so forlorn and sad, I, shuddering, felt its chilling gloom. The dryness of her eyes most plainly told her wounded heart had dried up the fountain of her tears, and that she had tried in vain to weep. Closely I drew her to "nin ki-gan" (my breast), and asked the cause. She sobbed aloud, "O, dear! dear! I can not find my loved waw-mawsh-kay-she. Nin segis tchi ki nibo! (I fear that he is dead!) Ki-mi etaw indowin (His only fault), which I have tried to check, sprang from kin sagia (his love) for me, and me alone. How could I, O, how could I have had the heart to grieve him so, when well I knew he was always the first to welcome and the foremost to defend! There has not been a time since he was ma-das-so gi-sis (ten moons) old he would not have given his life for mine; but he is gone, and all the fault is my own." I tried to cheer her wounded heart, but pressing both her hands against my breast, she said in her childlike grief, "Do-dam maw-tchawn (Do go away). Leave me alone." I went outdoors, a multitude of curious thoughts rushing through my staggered brain. To explore the tangled wilderness of jealousy in vain I tried, and wondered much if after all it might not be an offspring of true love in wedlock born; for, in spite of reason and all my sympathy for the dearest darling of "nin-o-daw" (my heart), who, sorrowing, mourned her treasure lost, I must here confess I wished, and almost prayed, "waw-mawsh-kay-she" never would come back.

While musing there a while I stood, Loda's mother came and said, "Pokagon, I know full well how you feel, but if you knew how Loda's o-daw (heart) for years has been bound up in that deer, and how he has watched and ever stood ready to defend our home, you would not blame the girl, but pity her. You must, too, remember that our race have always taught that the white deer is sacred, and that has a wonderful influence on the minds of our children." I simply gave reply, "Do you think I had best go in and try to console her?" "No, no," she said, "I think it would be better for you to go and stay with Kawbenaw tonight, and return in the morning; that will give her time to reflect upon the loss of her deer as connected with you and herself."

I left for Kawbenaw's at once. On my way, as I rounded a high hill facing the south, I noticed peeping through the fallen leaves a small pink flower. Kneeling down, as I raked away the leaves, I inhaled the sweet breath of "wa-bi-gon" (the trailing arbutus), our tribal flower of the north. Beautiful buds, bursting into bloom, surrounded the full-blown jewels, to deck the crown of spring. As I plucked it, I recalled to mind the story told me the previous night by Kaw-kee, who saw Loda, when a child, playing "owl with the crows," wearing a wreath of these beautiful flowers. On reaching the old trapper's hut, I was welcomed with a spirit that assured me the old man was really glad that I had come. He was in the best of spirits, and seeing the flowers, said, "Well! Well! Osh-kin-awe (young man), how did you learn that Loda believed those flowers came direct from the hands of Ki-je Man-i-towi-win (Divinity)?" I was seated on one of his finest robes, he taking another, reclined upon it close by. He then asked, "Do you know the Ottawa tradition of the creation of that beautiful flower?" I replied, "Kaw-win (I do not)." He then related the following tradition, in which I became so intensely interested, I almost lost sight of Loda, her deer, and Pokagon, too.

The Story

"Many, many moons ago there lived aki-wesi (an old man), alone in his lodge, beside sebin mash-kaw-ag (a frozen stream) in the forest. His locks were long and white with age. He was heavily clad in be-waw-ig (furs), for all the world was bi-boon (winter), sagi-po and mik-wam (snow and ice) everywhere. No-din (The winds) swept through the woods, searching every bush and tree for be-nesh-ig (birds) to chill, and chasing maw tchi man-i-tog (evil spirits) over high hills and through valleys deep and broad. And the old man went about vainly searching in the deep snow for pieces of wood to keep up the fire in the lodge.

"In despair he returned to the lodge, and sitting down by the last few dying coals, he cried to Ki-ji Manito (the God of heaven) that he might not perish. No-din-og (The winds) answered with a howl, and blew aside the door of his lodge, and there came in gwá-notch ban-ikwe (a most beautiful maiden); her cheeks were like wild, red roses; her eyes were large, and glowed like the eyes of kit-agaw-kons (the fawn's) in the moonlight; her hair was long and black as ka-gi-gi (the raven's) mi-gwan-og (feathers), and it touched the ground as she walked along; her hands were covered with willow oni mikog (buds), and on her head was a wreath of waw-bi-gon-og (wild flowers); her clothing was wish-co-bad mash-kos-sew (sweet grass) and ferns; her moccasins were wabi na-ba-gask (white lilies), and when she breathed, the air of the lodge became warm and fragrant. The old man said, 'Nind da-nis (My daughter), I am glad to see you. My lodge is cold and cheerless, yet it will shield you from the tempest of tibik (night). But do tell me who you are, coming into my lodge in such strange clothing? Come, sit here, and tell me of nind-au-kee (thy country) and nin gash-kia (thy victories), and I will tell thee of gwash-kwes-iwin (my exploits), for I am Manito (a spirit).'

"He then filled two o-paw-gan-og (pipes) with os-se-maw (tobacco), that they might smoke as they talked; and when the smoke had warmed the old man's tongue, he said: 'I am Manito. I blow my breath and the lakes become like boo-au-nag (flint), and the rivers stand still and bridge over.' The maiden answered: 'I breathe and the flowers spring up on all the plain.' The old man said: 'I breathe and sag-ipo (the snow) covers all aukee (the ground).' 'I shake my tresses,' returned the maiden, 'and warm rains fall from the clouds.' 'When I walk about,' answered the old man, 'leaves fade and fall from the trees. At my command the animals hide themselves in the ground, and the birds forsake the waters and fly away, for I am *Manito*.'

"The maiden made answer, 'When *I* walk about, the plants lift up their heads, and the naked trees cover themselves with green leaves without number, the birds come back, and all who see me sing for joy; music is everywhere.' And thus they talked, and the air became warmer and more fragrant in the lodge, and the old man's head drooped upon nin ka-ki-gan (his breast), and he slept.

"Then ke-sus (the sun) came back, and the bluebirds came to the top of the old man's lodge, and sang, 'Nin ni-bog-we! Nin ni-bog-we! (I am thirsty! I am thirsty!)' And seben (the river) replied, 'I am free; come and drink.' As the old man ni-baw-wind (slept), the maiden passed her hand above his head; he began to grow small, streams of water began to run out of o-don (his mouth), and very soon he was a small mass upon the ground, his clothing turned to withered leaves. Then the maiden, kneeling upon the ground, took from her bosom the most precious white flowers, and hid them about under the faded leaves, and breathing upon them, said: 'I give you all my virtues, and my sweetest breath, and all who would pick thee, shall do so upon bended knees.'

"Then the maiden moved away through the woods, and over the plain, and all the birds sang to her, and wherever she stepped, and *nowhere else*, grows our tribal flower, the trailing arbutus."

At the close of the old man's tradition of the origin of the trailing arbutus, I told him I had scarcely closed "nish-kin-jig" (my eyes) in two full days. He then threw over me, where inclined I lay, a well-tanned robe. Almost at once I fell soundly asleep, nor did I wake until some one shook my head, exclaiming, "Ta-gaw! Ta-gaw! (Halloo! Halloo!) Pogon! Pogon! Come, do get up." As I awoke, before me stood little Nonnee, saying, "Pogon! Pogon! *Why don't you get up?* Granddad has es-si-kan (a young raccoon) and o-me-me-og (wild pigeons) all roasted now—ready to eat." I arose, and after partaking of the rude but well-cooked morning meal, started on my return to Loda's home. The sun, though yet unseen, had painted the eastern sky a brilliant red. High in the air were multitudes of wild pigeons sweeping the heavens as far as eye could reach, moving in line after line, like columns of trained soldiers, southward to procure their morning meal.

All the twigs and branches of the grand old forest were thickly fringed with needled frost, forming a silvery screen through which the sunshine was sprinkled down, shedding the glory in the tree tops on the ground, filling my youthful soul with love for the Divine.

Stillness reigned almost supreme along the trail I passed, only broken now and then by "paw-kwe-a-moo" (the woodpecker) beating his chiseled bill into some decaying wood in search of food; or when some "bi-né" (partridge) on some prostrate tree, beat his rolling drum to entertain his lady love of early spring. I paused and listened to his oft-repeated drumbeats of love, poured forth in military style, and to myself I said, "Happy lover, no doubts disturb thy trusting heart, while fear and sore distrust are warring in my soul."

I reached the wigwam of my bride. All was quiet as the morning air. My beating heart was all the sound I heard; that, like a bird within a cage, beat the bars that held it fast. While standing before the door, a strange feeling held me there in bonds which none but a doubtful lover can ever know, and which no language can express.

While there I stood, Loda opened wide the door, bidding me come in. The chilling gloom of yesterday had left no impress on her face; but instead, the fondest smiles of maidenhood were plainly written there. I thought perhaps the deer had in the night returned, but soon I learned that he had not; then well I knew those smiles so sweet and bland, were all for me, and me alone. With mutual hearts we clasped each other round, and sealed again the marriage vow with concert kisses, imparting a thrill of joy so pure that only they who truly love can ever feel and fully understand.

VIII

W hen "wa-bi-gon-i gis-sis"[1] came, and mating birds were moving north in song, and wild flowers were blooming, and the trees were putting on their robes of green, I took the hand of my dear, young, loved Lonidaw, and she became my bride. No wedding cards were passed around, no gifts were made, no bells were rung, no feast was given, no priest declared us one. We only pledged our sincere faith before her mother and the King of Heaven. Our hopes, our joys were one.

Hand in hand, along an ancient trail we took our course until we reached a land of game. Here we paused, and like two mated birds that search and find a place to build "widj was-i-swan-og (their nests) of mud and straw) so we, beside "sa-gai-gan" (an inland lake), where towering woods embrowed its shore and flags, rushes, and "man-o-min" (wild rice) in plenty could be found, built our wigwam home of bark and poles. There, oft at morning dawn and evening tide, we fished from out our birch canoe; and that she might have more success than I, ofttimes I would bait well her hook and let my own go bare, then wonder why she caught more fish than I. And oft returning from the chase, weary and tired of carrying game, I'd follow down the trail upon a narrow neck of land that ran into the lake toward our home.

As I would emerge from out the woods upon the open shore, I never failed to see Lonidaw's erect and slender form on hasty run, to get the boat to bring me home. No "wob-isi" (swan) ever faster swam or more elegantly appeared than she, when bending to the oars, pushing "widg wig-was-tchi-man" (her birch canoe) across the swelling bosom of the lake. As she would approach me while waiting on the shore, I always hailed her, "Hoi (Hallo), o-gi-maw-kwe mit-i-gwa-ki (queen of the woods)."

No "as-a-wa-jonia" (gold) could buy the joy of admiration born in my soul, as I would catch the scornful glances of her eyes, almost concealed amid approving smiles. On our return across the lake she would cling to the oars and have me steer. I always felt her image in my heart, and loved to see it in the lake; and oft would ask if her feelings were akin to mine. Her only answer was an approving glance and

---

1. The moon of flowers and bloom corresponding to the last of May and the first of June.

downcast smile. Thus, happy in each other's love, we floated down life's stream, all unprepared for cataracts and rocks along the shore.

Some modest forest flowers were all the jewelry she ever wore; to keep a fresh supply of these, she taught "Zowan" (her dog), while yet young, to gather them from lake and land. In early spring time, at morning's dawn, with basket in his mouth, he would run into the deep, wild woods, fill it with the fairest flowers, then returning, drop them at her feet in great delight. And later on, at sunrise each day, when "na-bä-gāshk" (water-lilies) began to bloom, he would swim into the lake, and bring them to her by the mouthful, dripping with their diamonds of water.

Two years flew quickly by, when Olondaw, our first child, was born. The night he came, no man of skill, or neighbors, gathered at our home. Alone, in the presence of the Great Spirit and myself, Lonidaw went down to the gateway of death's dark valley, and brought forth our darling boy, together with a father's and a mother's crown, one for her, and one for me. As I beheld, in the first morning light, our cherished infant nestling on "o ka-ki-gan" (her breast), and saw Lonidaw smile in triumph as she gazed on me, my love, respect, and sympathy for her were all at sea without a shore. No morning press or busy tongues proclaimed that the child was born and mother doing well, but all about our woodland home wild birds and flowers rejoiced with us, and we were richly blessed, feeling the dear boy was sent of "Waw-kwi" (Heaven) to our wigwam, as a seal to our union, that it might not be broken; for if there is one holy tie of love more sacred than the rest, it is that a true-hearted husband feels for his dear wife when their first child is born.

Nearly three years more of pleasant life passed on, and a second child was given. It was late in "taw-kwa-kwo-pe" (autumn time); and the forest trees had cast aside their robes of green to combat with the winter's storm, when Hazeleye, our little girl, was born. No flowers anywhere were to be seen except upon the leafless branches of "pa-gan-i-mig" (the witch-hazel shrubs), which only blooms when winter blasts sweep through the woods. No singing birds were to be heard except "chin-dees" (the blue jays), with their discordant songs in mimicry of other birds long gone to their southern homes. On that cold, eventful night, no grandma came in sympathy to cheer; no embroidered skirts and blankets silken trimmed had been prepared to dress the little waif thrown naked on the world; but in furs Lonidaw had prepared and laid aside, as soft as "si-a-mo mis-se-gwan" (eider-down), we wrapped "osh-kï ä-bin'-od-jï" (the infant child). When morning, came Olondaw was shown the little stranger of the night. He gazed at her in wonder and surprise, then cautiously drew near and felt her silken fingers and her toes; then with one hand, smoothed down her dimpled cheeks, as if afraid of the result; growing bolder in his moves, at length he tried to touch her twinkling eyes, when she began to cry and sob as if her little heart would break! Alarmed, he, too, began to weep, and ran away and hid. Zowan then came to see the strange intruder of the night. He viewed her with a jealous eye. No look of welcome did he give; but sullenly, with downcast look and drooping tail, slowly walked away, and lay down beside the boy in his hiding-place, as though both were crowded out by the coming little stranger. But few days passed by, and the little boy's heart became bound up in the precious little girl. He loved her as he loved himself, and oft would grieve because his lap was all too small to hold the little pet. As time rolled on, the dog became convinced she had not come to crowd him out, but to caress and fondle him.

No stranger "min-ons" or "an-i-mosh" (cat or dog), or "aw-es-si" (animal) of any size, while he was near, dare approach "we-bi-son" (the hammock) where she lay, for fiercely he would pounce upon them. As time passed on the little elf, in elegance of make and mold of body and of limb, was the very image of Lonidaw. As years came and went, both grew beautifully fair; and as they entered into their childish sports that seemed almost endless, so our love for them grew almost boundless. "Mit-ig-wab" and "pik-wak" (The bow and arrow), born in the boy's heart, he worked into shape, and with his cunning hands would let fly the shaft that seldom failed to hit the mark.

His little sister, all delighted with the sport, laid aside "midg a-nak-an-ashk" (her rushes), braid, and "a-waw-is" (doll)[2] to join him as a rival in his sport. With pure Indian pride he taught her how to bend the bow and direct the arrow in its course. In great delight she watched him work from out "mit-i-gwa-bak" (the hickory tree), with ax and knife, arrows and bow. And that each might know their own, her dart he feathered white, and his he colored red. Our palefaced neighbors,

---

2. I am frequently asked by white girls: "Say, Mr. Pokagon, do Indian children play with dolls as we do?" My answer is, "No, not exactly as you do; for when *our* little girls have dolls, some are boys, as well as girls. And they never leave *their* dolls lying on their backs until they get all tired out, but change them from side to side so they may have sweet dreams and sleep well."

hearing of their sport, often gathered near our door, and placing cents in crotches of the limbs, gave them as prizes to the child who would first shoot them down at space of twenty feet or more; but few shots were made that did not the copper coins bring down.

One day while they were wandering by the lake, "wab-i-si" (a swan) lit in a wild rice cove close by, near the shore; as quick as thought each two successive arrows sent at the giant bird. In vain she tried to rise in air, but could not, for two arrows, transfixed in her neck, stuck fast. Zowan, the dog, rushed into the lake and brought the dying swan to shore. Like heroes, in triumph each seized the prey, fearing the prize so nearly won might yet be lost. Each in haste withdrew an arrow from her neck, the boy exclaiming, "I killed bi-nes-si (the bird)! I killed bi-nes-si! See my arrow with feather red!" The girl responding, said: "I killed her, too! See my arrow with feather white!" and both rejoiced together in true native style.

I yet love to recall the little pets as home they came that day with the big, white swan tied to a pole across their shoulders thrown.

One day "me-kat-e-wik'-wan-e" (a priest) in royal robes came to our wigwam home to see the little archers try their skill. To his surprise they knocked down fifty coins, which he placed at space of thirty feet or more, and only missed but one. After this he often came to see us, and requested that we would give consent to send Olondaw, at his expense, away to the white man's school, that he might become learned, great, and good, and thereby be of great service to our race. At length I gave him my consent, but Lonidaw shuddered at the thought; in fact, she grieved over it *most* bitterly. "For," said she, "when but a child my girlish curiosity often led me to take pan-ad-gag (young birds), nearly grown, from their nests, and when I placed them back with cautious, tender care, they never failed as soon as my hand was lifted from waw-sis-swan (the nest) to spring therefrom, and fall fluttering to the ground, and in the night time chill and die."

When the boy was twelve years old, Lonidaw reluctantly gave her consent that he might go away to school, but not until she exacted a solemn promise from the priest that he should be carefully cared for, and strongly guarded against the intoxicating cup, that deadly enemy of our race. The night before Olondaw left, Lonidaw dreamed she was near the wigwam of her childhood days, and that in a familiar bush by the trailside she found two young "au-pe-tchig" (robins) in their nest, nearly grown. She just touched one gently with her hand. It leaped from out the nest chirping a wild alarm, and fell fluttering to the ground. The parent birds, distracted, came flying all about uttering mourning notes of deepest sorrow. She sought the young bird to place it back into its nest again; but in her astonishment she saw it moving as if by measured tread on tiptoe hop, with drooping wings, toward a monstrous "gin-e-big" (snake) with open mouth, that was drawing the young bird by some unseen charm into "pe-kar ni-o-wib" (the jaws of death). In haste she grasped "mit-a-gos" (a club) to beat the reptile off, but as she struck with all her might it seized the bird; when lo, to her surprise, the snake within its jaws held fast, not the bird, but the living skeleton of her son, struggling to escape. The boy in terror cried, "Ne-gaw-she! io Ne-gaw-she! (My mother! oh, my mother!) do save ne kwi-wi-sens (your boy)." Screaming, she awoke, and told "nina-baw-tan" (her dream) and said, "I never have believed in ena'-baw-tan-og (dreams), but this one seems so real, I do believe with all nin-o-daw (my heart) it has been sent of wa-kwi (heaven) as a warning not to send our boy to ki-ki-no-am-a-dig wau-be-au-ne-ne (the school of the white man)."

That day O-lon-daw, with the priest, left our home to be gone three years at school. I visited him once each year while there. Lonidaw saw him not again until three years had passed. He then returned. It was early morning. He was dressed in a suit of blue. I stood outside the open door of our wigwam as he came running through the yard with Zowan, who met him first, close at his heels with sparkling eyes and wiggling tail to welcome his return. Hastily he grasped my hands in his, then ran into the house clasping his mother in his arms, impressing many kisses on her cheek, which she repaid, bathing them in tears. My heart was overjoyed to see the mother and son in such sweet embrace. But all at once I heard an awful scream, and looking up, saw Lonidaw unclasp her hold and backward quickly step, and sobbed aloud; and in her native tongue she said: "Ne-gris! ne-gris! (My son! my son!) waw nind aian api-ne? waw nind aian api-ne? (what have you done? what have you done?)" I gazed upon our darling boy, while from his lips came this response: "Nin-gaw waw ki-wab? (My mother, what do you see?) io! waw ki-wab! (oh! what *do you* see?)" She gazed into his face, and then at me, weeping aloud, she said, "Nin ban-a-den-dan! Nin ban-a-den-dan! (He is lost! He is lost!) From out o-don (his mouth) I smell o-taw-a-gam-eg (the dragon's) breath!" Our boy moved not; he was as pale as marble, and as dumb. At length I said, "My son, have you any fire-water about you?" As quick as sight he drew a bottle from his coat, dashing it against the floor, saying in broken tones, "I'll never, never touch it again;" and falling on the floor, he wept long and bitterly. Lonidaw and I, most sorely grieved, quietly walked outdoors, Zowan following with head drooped low, as if ashamed of Olondaw, and in sympathy with us. Standing in silence there a while, she said, "O, dear! dear! how I do wish we had obeyed the warning dream sent by Ki-je Man-i-to (the Great Spirit). I know that monstrous gin-e-big (snake) I saw tib-ik (the night) before he left for school, holding fast his living skeleton, will surely swallow him alive."

Hoping to soothe her grieving heart, I said, "Lonidaw, he is so broken down I hardly think he will touch it again." Looking me in the face, she said, "Simaw, those words, 'I'll never touch it again,' are meaningless to me. So said nin noss (my father) time and time again, and well thou knowest, for I have told thee how he continued to fall down and worship aw-es-si (the beast) until he cursed ki-wish and a-bin-od-ji (his wife and child), cursed himself, and cursed Ki-ji Man-i-to (his God), and died." After the first excitement had somewhat abated, we went back into the house. Lonidaw said, "Now, o-gwis-san (my son), you must tell me who it was that first gave you that deadly pit-chib-o-win (poison)." He replied, "No one gave it to me." "Well, then," said she, "how did you get it?" He replied, "The second week at school some boys about my size got me to go with them 'bottle-hunting,' as they called it. They went into the back allies about the town, picking up ish-kot-e-waw-be o-mo-dens (whisky bottles) that had been thrown away by drinking men, these they would fill with ni-bish (water), drink it, and sell the bottles. Ik-we-sens ki-we (The boys said) I could find more bottles in an hour than three white boys could in three hours, and called me the "little red-skin hunter." And so it was by min-an-dan-win (smelling) and min-ik-we-win (drinking) the rinsing water that I began to like it, and after a while I wanted it so awfully bad I could think of nothing else. Then I would go o-mo-dens gi-os-se-win (bottle-hunting). A big boy used to take my bottle-money and buy whisky for me on the halves, as he called it; as he said I could not buy it, because I was an Indian boy. Now, what I have told you, we-gi-mind (mother), is as true as I live." Then, looking her square in the face for the first time while making the confession, he said, "I think it's awful mean, don't you, to throw away bottles of fire-water for boys to learn to get drunk on?"

IX

I do not wish to bleed my own heart, or sadden yours; suffice it to say, as darkness succeeds the meteor's sudden glare, so his young life went out and left us in the midnight of despair.

Dear little Hazeleye alone was left us then; that sweet rosebud, just opening into maidenhood, the very image of her mother, was our only hope, and as our hearts were bound up in hers, we consoled ourselves with the assurance that she was so isolated from the alluring serpent born of the white man that she was safe from all harm that might come from such a source.

But soon, alas! we were compelled to learn the bitter truth, that no one is safe from the destroying hand of that soulless enemy, fed and fattened by the human race, so long as he is provided a home among them. One day, while I was absent on "gi-os-se" (a hunt), and Hazeleye was fishing on the lake, two drunken "gi-go-ike win" (fishermen) rowed their boat with such recklessness, they ran into "nin-tchi-man" (her bark canoe), which was broken and capsized, throwing her out into sa-gai-gan. Lonidaw, standing on the shore, saw the crash and heard "o-be-bawg" (her scream). She wildly cried, "Maw-and-gia! Maw-and-gia! Do-dam maw-and-gia nind-jan-is! (Save! Save! Do save my child!)" But, paralyzed by that deadly drug, those drunken men, though white, could not see the living diamond struggling in the lake for life, but centered all their powers on that false diamond of the alluring wine, of which they drank with idiotic "ba-piwin" (laughter), while yet the lake was bubbling with her dying breath, and never raised "onind-jima" (a hand) to save the child.

Lonidaw, in her frenzy, plunged into the flood, and swam desperately, as none but a mother could, to save a drowning child.

Zowan, returning home from the hunt in my advance in time to hear the screams of Hazel-eye, rushed into the lake, and reached the wrecked canoe just at the time Lonidaw did; with plaintive cries and head erect, with anxious looks, to right, to left, and down into the lake he swam around the wrecked canoe, once, twice, thrice, then pausing, said in a most plaintive howl: "Your child can not be saved." All hope now gone, Lonidaw strangling, struggling, sank beneath the waves, then rose again; then sank and rose again.

The dog swam quickly to her relief. Soon as she felt his touch, by chance she clutched her hands into the long hair of "o-no-gan" (his hips), with that grip a drowning man clings to a straw. The dog, with all his might and main, pulled for the shore; nor did he pause until he drew her safe upon the land. During these heart-rending scenes, I was returning from the chase with a heavy deer across my shoulders thrown, pondering in my heart how warmly I should be greeted by wife and child on my return. As I was nearing home along the common trail on the terrace of the lake, Zowan met me on the run with whimpering cry, then gave the saddest howl I ever heard. It shocked my nerves, for well I knew he said, "Do hurry home." Quickly I threw my burden down, and followed him almost on "mi-gi-si" (eagle) wings.

He led me to the shore where Lonidaw unconscious lay. Her drenched clothes, capsized canoe upon the lake, and Hazeleye nowhere to be seen impressed me with the awful thought that she was drowned in the lake.

Clasping Lonidaw in my arms, supposing she was dead, I carried her into our wigwam, and on mats of rushes she had lately made I laid her down. Soon she began to gasp for breath, and then began to breathe with a strange rattle in "ok-we-gan" (her throat). During that long night of sorrow, amid sighs and groans, sobs and tears, she told me the sad story of our dear Hazeleye.

When morning came, she was not herself. At times she would say in her mother tongue, "Sa-gá-i-gán ma-man-gásh-ka (The waves run awful high), mash-káw-is-sín bim-á-da-gä (it is hard to swim with Hazeleye). Nin gós-a-bí! Nin gós-a-bí! (I sink! I sink!) Bín-das ké-ji-dín mít-i-gó tchi-män (Bring the boat quickly)!" And again she would say, "Nin ín-en-dám-o-wín nin-id-jan-íss nin-máw-and-ji-ä (I thought it was my child that I had saved), má-ka nin mi-kä-wa an-i-mosh nin maw-and-ji-ä (but I find it is the dog that I have saved)!" After an elapse of several weeks, which seemed stretched out into years, as I sat beside her, she looked up to me, clothed in her right mind, and said, "Pokagon, see ke-sus (the sun) is sinking low; while it is going down, I shall pass into manito aukee we-de (the spirit land beyond). You have always been kind to me, yet I must bid you farewell until we meet beyond tchi-be-gam-mig (the grave), where no alluring beverage of nib-o-win (death) shall curse us any more. But, promise me, when I am gone you will mi-gass (fight), so long as you shall live, against tchi ni-boma (that destroyer) of our race. Against that heartless tyrant, whose murderous hands are stained with the blood of my dear father, while I was but a child. Against that tyrant, who, by his acts of cruelty, crushed out my dear mother's life and left me an orphan bride. Against that tyrant, who, shackling, led astray sa-si-ka-win (our first-born), and murdered him while yet a youth. Against that tyrant fiend, who, not satisfied when he had destroyed o-gwis-san (our only son), sought us out in our humble, woodland home, and while we thought no danger nigh, with ruthless hands, cast our dear Hazeleye, who knew no wrong, into the chilling waters of the lake, where she sleeps unseen, except by Him who gave her birth. Against that tyrant, who, by such acts of cruelty, shocked the tender life-cords of my being, and forced me to this couch of death. Will you thus promise?" I answered, "Lonidaw, the Great Spirit being my helper, I will." She whispered faint and low, "Nind in-em-dam aw-nam-ya ki (I will pray for thee)." I heard one deep "kwan-a-mo-win" (sigh). Slower and slower she breathed, until she ceased. "Ke-sus" (The sun) had set. I pressed my hand close to her side until I felt the last pulsation of "nin-o-daw" (her heart). Then, oh, then, I knew that she was dead.

Trembling with icy chills, I left her side and sat upon the threshold of the open door. I saw through bitter tears "waw-bi-gon-og" (the flowers) along our wigwam trail, that she had planted with her own hands, droop their heads, and weep with me. I heard the wild wood birds, all about the lake, chanting her farewell requiem; and "ti-kow" (the waves) joining the refrain, murmured, "Farewell, O-gi-maw-kwa mit-igwa-ki (Queen of the Woods)." As "tebikad" (night) came on, "ish-ko-te odg-i tching wang" (the fire-fly meteors) flashed on every side, reminding me of guardian angels sent from the eternal world to guide "o manito gi-we" (her spirit home).

X

On her funeral day, no relatives in sable robes appeared, no hearse, with ostrich feathers crowned, bore her form away.

But native hunters of the wild, who oft had shared the bounties of her home, they dug her grave at early morn; then came with fragrant woodland flowers, and on her casket laid them.

They came with blankets of pure white about their shoulders thrown, and with moccasins of deer-hide upon their feet, while, with uncovered heads and muffled tread, slowly they bore her from the door away.

A Christian teacher and I next to them came, while in our rear, true-hearted neighbors followed on. Zowan started as a mourner, too, but some one, unconscious of his grieving heart, jerked him about and drove him home. Tenderly they carried her along the winding trail, under lofty archways of giant trees, until they reached her last resting-place, which she in life had chosen. And there, among the evergreen trees, upon a beautiful headland, near the shore of our forest lake, in sight of the waters that covered our dear Hazeleye, we gathered, and there sadly consigned her to the grave, dropping therein modest forest flowers which she in life oft wore and much admired; and, as we listened in silent prayer, to the solemn words: "Earth to earth and dust to dust," a little dusky maiden of our band, who lately had been taught the Saviour's love, and knew Lonidaw well, all unbidden sang,—

> *"Asleep in Jesus, blessed sleep*
> *From which none ever wake to weep;*
> *A calm and undisturbed repose,*
> *Unbroken by the last of foes."*

The closing words were scarcely sung, when from the shore across the lake, in childlike tenderness, the song again was sung, and again and again was repeated from shore to shore, weaker and weaker, until it died away the merest whisper in our ears.

In tears of gratitude, and with a heart of prayer, I blessed the little maiden there. One by one the friends forsook the spot, leaving me there alone to commune with the spirit of my departed Lonidaw. Kneeling beside her grave, I breathed a silent prayer to the Great Spirit, that she might be received into the arms of Hazeleye in his kingdom beyond.

Then I arose, and sorrowfully started homeward, saying in my heart, "All this trouble now weighing down my soul, has fallen upon me by reason of that curse, dealt out to our race by the hands of white men." And as I reflected upon it, the despot rose up before me like a thing of beauty, as if to tempt even me in "nin kash-ken-dam-owin" (my sorrow), and I cried out in the anguish of my soul: "O, thou wretch! Pull aside that gold-gilt veil, which now conceals thy wicked face, and speak no more to me with flattering lips and lying tongue, that all may see thee as thou art, and shun thee as a viper." I reached my lonely home. No crape was hung upon the latch-string of the door. No friends had gathered there to cheer the mourning heart on its return. Zowan gave one plaintive howl, then rushing forward, met me on the trail, impressing many kisses on my cheek. I could not have the heart to ward him off, for well I knew he told his love and sympathy by honest acts, and not by flattering words. How different with our petted cat. She, all unmoved, lay by the door quietly purring her time away, as if Lonidaw had not died. The dog, ashamed of her unfeeling heart, drove her quickly from the door. I went to the wigwam, expecting to enter in, but passed by it, for a shrinking feeling of dread to enter came over me. With faithful Zowan at my side, I walked slowly back to Lonidaw's grave, and sat down upon an old, mossy log close beside it. Let only those who have lost dear friends attempt to tell, or realize what then I felt. My sad heart, whispering, said: "How unfeeling, strange, and droll it seems, that she who I have so much loved for many years, and watched so tenderly so long, should now be abandoned and consigned to the cold earth. Zowan tried to soothe my broken heart by wiping away the tears I shed. Poor fellow! He had a double sorrow. Mourning to see me weep, and grieving because his best friend was dead. Laying my hand upon his head, I said: "Zowan, kin-ish-kwatch waw-bi-gon (you have gathered your last flowers) for Lonidaw." He started up as if she had called his name, and bounding to "sa-gi-i-gan" (the lake), plunged in, soon returning with his mouth full of water-lilies of pure white, dropping them upon her grave. Patting "kish-ti-gwan" (his head), I gave him an approving look. Again and again he went and came, until her grave was almost covered with the beautiful flowers, which glistened like "a-gon gi-si-win" (snow in the sunshine) among the trees. With "nish-kin-jig" (my face) pressed to my hands, and "bim-in-ik-og" (elbows) resting on "ki-gi-di-og" (my knees), there in meditation deep I sat, until aroused by the sweet voice of a child; and looking up, saw advancing toward me a little boy and girl of the white race. Just then they paused as if afraid, turned about, and on tiptoe were walking quietly away. Arising to "ni-si-don" (my feet), I said, "Please stop, little pets, and tell me what you want." Turning about, the little girl replied, "We came across the big lake to put dese on her grave," at the same time each holding up a wreath of flowers, "but we be afraid of de big dog." "He will not hurt you," I replied. "Bless you, your dear little hearts. Come right along here, and see the flowers the dog himself has brought. He is glad you have brought some, too."

The little ones then stepped cautiously forward, eying the dog, while they lay the wreaths upon her grave. I said, "Did you know Lonidaw." Quickly the girl replied, "O, yes we did. Las' fall we get los', we did, and find her home; we were mos' starved to death, and she gave us lots and lots to eat, she did. Then she take her boat and bring us home, she did—way 'cross the big lake; we tho't the lake had turned 'round, but it hat n't, though." I then said, "Do you know me?" "O, yes," said she, "we have seen you go by our house carrying big deer good many times, and ma and pa do bof say you have been gone so much the squaw woman get lonesome, and die she did." I thanked them kindly for their tokens of love for Lonidaw, when they, bidding me good-by, were soon out of sight. Late in the afternoon, reluctantly I left the sacred spot; I had taken but few steps when I paused, as it occurred to me no lettered stones would ever rise above her last resting-place. So retraced my steps, and on a tree at the head of her grave I cut her name and age, thirty-four, adding, "Queen of the Woods."

Then in pensive mood, slowly I passed down to the margin of the lake, following along the shore, until I reached the old landing-place close beside our home. The sun was just going down, and twilight began to spread its misty curtain o'er the wild. The lake was smooth as polished glass, the shore line and the trees were seen as plainly in the lake as on the land, while in the air above and lake beneath, bats, like butterflies, flitted about; "jash-wan-i-bi-si" (the swallows) in wider circles flew; "tib-ik-gib-wa-se" (the night-hawks) high above them sailed, rising at times as if to scale "gi-jig" (the sky), then headlong descending like "tchin-gwan-og" (meteors) from above, with a strange, hollow sound; while all around the lake the whippoorwills, whose only songs are but their names, a chattering concert gave; and later on, to add new glories to the scene, deep in the lake as heaven is high, appeared the galaxy of glittering stars set like diamonds in the vault of blue. All nature seemed to do her best to cheer my broken heart. While there upon a rock I sat, at intervals I could faintly hear, far in the south, low muttering thunders that seemed to vibrate with the gloomy feelings of my soul. While sitting there, with Zowan beside me, my spirit flew across the lake, following on my hunting trails of former days, surveyed the grounds where many deer had fallen by my bow, then homeward came with heavy buck across my shoulders thrown; again, standing on the open beach where I had often stood before gazing at Lonidaw bending to the oars. Then again, as she approached me on the shore, I cried, "Hoi! (Halloo!) O-gi-maw-kwe Mit-i-gwa-ki! (Queen of the Woods)." Again I saw her approving smile mixed with her modest frown. Again, a noble stag with antlers broad, into the boat I threw, while in myself I sprung. Again I felt her image in my soul, and viewed it in the lake. Arriving at our landing-place, as quick as thought my spirit with its body joined. Just then a sudden flash of lightning lit up the lake and all the shore, followed by the deafening thunder's roar, that rolled away, but to return from the surrounding hills with a more subdued and solemn sound. Zowan whined as if shocked, pressing his nose between my knees.

Quickly springing to my feet, I rushed into the wigwam to avoid the storm without, only to arouse the slumbering storm of sorrow in my soul. The lightning's repeated glare lighted the trophies of the chase that hung about the room, and all therein. At times, like jarring, heavy bars of steel, the thundering sound rolled on, as though the clouds were paved with bricks of steel, and chariots of war were being driven in great haste over them, while ever and anon there came a sound as though some mighty car had broken through the pavement of the clouds, crushing down the forest where it fell. Again, I would imagine that perhaps outraged humanity, long crushed to earth, had risen in its might, and was engaged in one great final battle against the legions of King Alcohol, and that all the artillery of the world was being brought forward to engage in the dire conflict. At intervals, the blinding flash and deafening roar would cease, as though contending armies were preparing for a general advance all along their lines. Then the awful silence would be broken by the roar of cannon, and the rattle of musketry, shaking heaven and earth, followed by the clash of steel, as when charging columns meet. And as I listened in grief and awe, I cried out to "Manito" (the Lord) of the storm: "Howl on! While yet Lonidaw lived, the lightning of thine eyes, and the deep-toned thunder of nin gi-git-owin (thy voice) did cause her poor enfeebled frame to tremble as a-saw-di ani-bish (an aspen leaf), but now I challenge thee to speak with all thy power and majesty. Thou canst not disturb her last repose."

At "a-bit-a-tib-i-kad" (midnight), where an hour before the clouds hung like a blazing pall above, now unnumbered diamonds, polished by the storm, a twinkling concert gave. All seemed hushed to rest, except the roaring brook close by; that, like some furious serpent, rushed along, with wave-like motion, lashing the underbrush on either side beneath its mighty weight.

And "sa-ga-i-gan" (the lake), that lay as quiet as a sleeping lamb at set of sun, now like some maddened beast tormented in his cage, in fury lashed the bars that held it fast. It was the midnight of my soul. No diamonds glittered there. The storm still swept across the nerves of life, and chilled my throbbing heart and brain. Alone in my wigwam with the old, faithful dog at my side, I knelt and poured out my soul in prayer and tears to the Great Spirit. I told him all about how Olondaw, my only son, had been murdered by the demon of the alluring cup born of another race, and how my dear Hazeleye, without any fault of hers, while fishing on the lake, was thrown therein by drunken men, and, though long we searched, her body never could be found.

I told him how my dear Lonidaw, who he gave me, became broken-hearted over the downfall and loss of our dear boy, and how she fell a victim to despair, and died because of the sudden death of our dear Hazeleye, leaving me wretched and alone. I told him not only of my own family and kin, but how my band and tribe were falling before the intoxicating cup, like leaves before the autumn's blast; and that bad "waw-be-au-ne-ne" (white men), who appeared to love "se-wan" (money) more than "o-tchi-tchag-wan" (their own souls), had pressed to "nin o-don" (our lips) the alluring beverage of hell, and after having ruined many of "nin osh-ke-maw" (our young men) and "nin aw-ki-we-seg" (our old men), had most wickedly published to the world that the red man would barter all he possessed on earth for "ish-kot-e-wa-be" (fire-water). I told him all about the promise made my loved Lonidaw, while she lay dying, that I would war against the monster so long as I should live, and prayed for strength and courage to attack greedy "maw-in-gawn" (the wolf) wherever found; and asked that he would, in some way, or somehow, personify the influence for evil of strong drink upon the palefaced race, as compared with its effects upon my own people. I fell "ni-baw" (asleep) while on "nin gi-dig" (my knees) in prayer; and in "na-gwi-i-dis te-be-cut" (the visions of the night)

I was lifted high above Au-kee, and there on steady "nin-gwi-gan" (wing), like "tchi-tchi-gig-waw-ne" (the osprey) watching for some victim of the deep, so I, balancing in mid-air, watched unnumbered multitudes of the palefaced race, which filled the wide, extended "taw-awd-ino" (plain) beneath. While wondering there, I gazed. I beheld marching among the mighty throng the most vicious-looking creature my eyes ever beheld; no brush of "mau-tchi man-ito" (the devil) could paint his wicked "kin-jig" (face); no language of "Ki-tchi-isk-u-to" (hell) could describe it. About his form was wrapped "wa-be-yon" (a blanket) with "an-ong-og" (the stars) and stripes thereon, among which was outlined an American "mi-gi-si" (eagle), with wings half spread, while across "ni-kat-i-gwan" (his forehead) deeply impressed, I read, "United States and City Seals." Under "nin ki-tchi-nik" (his right arm), half concealed, he held a bundle of poisonous "gin-e-big-og" (serpents) which writhed, convulsed, and hissing, snapped "wi-big-og" (their teeth), and escaping in great numbers, they ran like "ni-ki-bi-win" (a flood) in all directions, still the numbers held grew none the less. In "ki tchi-nig" (his right hand) he held a scorpion whip, which he wielded with such skilled force, that it sounded more like the report of a gun than the snap of a lash. Thus clothed with civic and national emblems, the despot marched forth on "ki-mi-gan" (his trail), defiantly treading, with feet of steel, upon beating human hearts that were yet struggling in "mis-kwi" (their own blood). "Nin-o-daw" (my heart) almost ceased to beat as I saw the defiant despot marching toward beautiful homes, drawing his mantle closer about him so as to conceal the snakes and scorpions hidden there, as if "kawin a-ga-tchi-win" (no shame) "nin in-en-o-win" (his conscience) stung, with brazen face he boldly entered in the homes of sunshine and of smiles. Some, when they met him, grasped "o-nindg" (his hand), as though he were a friend, or brother, or some benefactor of their race. Others, when they saw him, closed their doors against him, saying to the monster man, "If thou will keep aloof from us, we will not disturb thee;" but, regardless of their wishes, he forced his way into many homes, blighting the fairest of the household.

Some fled away before his presence and hid themselves in fear; but he searched *them* out, letting loose his snakes and scorpions, which pursued many of them to disgrace and "ni-bo-win" (death).

Others there were, who, with frantic cries, swarmed about the monster man, on right, on left, in front and rear, like birds about the robber "ke-kek" (hawk) that flies away clutching a dying "pe-nan-ja" (nestling) in its claws.

Frequently they would tear his royal robes apart, exposing to public gaze the snakes and vipers hidden there. Anxiously I asked, "Who are those men and women so *desperate* in their attack?" A voice replied, "They are the true lovers of humanity, and the fathers and mothers whose sons and daughters the despot has destroyed." I then looked with greater care, and saw to my astonishment, many boys of tender age, being caught like "ke-go" (fish) with his alluring "od-ji" (bait), and as "minons" (the cat) plays with its prey until it dies, so this monster played with them, until they drooped and died, like charmed insects that rush at night into "ish-ko-te" (a flame of fire); and as I listened, I heard the wails of "ban-i-kweg" (maidens) for "sa-ag-i-wed-og" (their lovers), "i-kweg" (wives) for "o-na-be-man-og" (their husbands), and "kit-i-sig" (parents) for "on-id-jan-is-sang" (their children), all alike before the Christian altar, agonizing in prayers and tears of blood, that the old dragon who dealt out "ish-kot-e-waw-boo" (the fire-water) of hell and murder might be forever destroyed from off the face of the earth.

As I was thoughtfully considering in my heart "mi-chi-kash-ken-dam-o-win" (the great sorrow) brought upon the dominant race, as well as my own, by the beverage of "a-gatch-i-win achi ni-bo-win" (shame and death). I saw along *every* trail where the monster wretch had been, staggering, stalwart young men, and old men with haggard looks, faces blotched, and eyes bloodshot and bleared, shrieking and pleading for help, pointing, with trembling fingers, in mortal agony, whispering, as they wildly gazed, "See! See! the ghosts of hell, panther-like, are crouching to pounce upon me."

Some, in mad delirium, shook lizards from their clothes. Others, in desperation, tore coiled serpents from their necks, and strangling, prostrate fell, and there, like dying wolves with poisoned "pik-wak" (arrows) pierced, foam at the mouth.[1] With laugh and cry, with curse and prayer at each succeeding breath, the terror and the pity of the crowd. Their dearest friends tried to soothe their agonies and fears, but all in vain. Before those anxious ones "Nit-aw-ge-win me-me" (the mourning dove of Hope) on tiptoe stood, with fluttering wings, to take its flight, while "Ka-ga-gi-bawn a-den-dam" (the raven of Despair)

---

1. When thoughtfully considered, there is nothing so pitiful to behold as a man in the last stages of the delirium tremens. Who sees it once, never wishes to see it again.

flapped its wings in their faces, screaming in "o-to-og" (their ears), "Too late! Too late! Alas, too late!"

Among the drunkards in the throng, a few I saw whose breath took fire within, while from their mouths and nostrils issued blue-like sulphurous flames, cremating them alive, leaving but charred and blackened bones to tell what they had been.[2] As I breathed in the sickening odors that scented all the air, gasping for breath I cried from out the depth of my pitying "ó-tchi-tcha-gó-maw" (soul), "O, Thou who seeth and knoweth ka-ki-naw (all things), hide Pokagon from such a scene of misery and death! He can endure no more and live. He is now fully satisfied the mighty Kraken is *not* in the sea, *but on* the land, and that the dreaded monster regards not age, race, or condition, but tramples down alike both chief and king; the white man in his palace, and the red man in his hut; alike the gray-haired sire, and the little son of tender years."

---

2. It is well authenticated that many persons addicted to drinking great amounts of stimulants, have taken fire by spontaneous combustion. Among that number is one Indian. He was reported from Alaska less than one year since. It appears it may happen at almost any age, but most of the cases are of persons advanced in years. The victims have generally been very corpulent; the extremities, such as the legs, hands, feet, and cranium have escaped fire. Water, instead of extinguishing the fire, gives it more activity, as happens when fat is burned. It is supposed that the carbon of the alcohol deposited in the fatty parts of the human system produces the effect.

SIMON POKAGON

XI

Being fully convinced that sorrow and desolation followed everywhere in the footsteps of strong drink, I recalled the dying request of my dear, lost Lonidaw, and again sealed the sacred contract within my heart, that I would raise "mi-gas" (the war-whoop) of alarm against that old dragon, not only in behalf of my own race, but in behalf of the white race as well, so long as life should last. But the solemn thought came home to "nin tchi-tchag" (my soul), What can I do in my "kit-i-mag-is-i-win" (poverty),—I, a child of the forest? Already I am broken down by loss, care, and anxiety, feeling that the wigwam of my soul is unlocked; that the latch-string has been pulled; that life's latch has been lifted, leaving the door ajar. But a few more days, and like "a-bod-ash-kwa'-ne-shi'" (the dragonfly) that lies entombed in mud and mire through "bibon" (winter's) reign, when "sig-wan" (springtime) comes, rises to the surface of "ni-bish" (the water), and bursting the shroud that confines it, flies away, so shall I go forth out of the wigwam of mortality, to join "nos-sog" (my fathers) and "nin-gag" (my mothers) in the land beyond; yet I am determined, while crossing the threshold of life's open door, that I will raise "in-we-win" (my voice), though feeble it may be, and cry out most bitterly against that beast, to whom the red man and the white man are alike a race "a-waw-kan-og" (of slaves); against that beast who is no enemy outside our lines, but a traitor within our camp; against that beast that fondles and embraces, but to strangle; against that beast, who, petting, "o-din-di-win" (kisses) but to bite and poison, like the snake without the warning hiss.

Pokagon believes with all his heart, that if some dire "nib-o-win" (contagion) should sweep our land as disastrous to health and life as the alluring cup, that those wild scenes which were enacted in London during the great plague there, would be repeated here. Business would be paralyzed; social gatherings cease; no church bell would be rung in all "au-kee" (the land); many would forsake home and fiee to "wad-jew-og" (the mountains); others to "kitch-i-gam-og" (the high seas), and all that human effort could do, would be done to prevent "ni-bo-win" (the deadly disease). My dear white friends, Pokagon is fully convinced; yes, he doth know that this fire-water of "an-am-ak-am-ig" (hell) should give you greater cause for alarm than any "ni-bo-win" (disease) that has ever visited our shores. It not only destroys more lives by a hundredfold, but is also the father and mother of want, disease, shame, crime, and death. The microbes of the social plague invade alike the homes of the rich and poor, of the learned and the unlearned; and all unsought, swarm like maddened "a-mog" (wasps) about the trusting "i-kwe" (bride), the young mother and the infant at her breast, impregnating all alike with the virus from its alluring "on-a-gans nish-i-waw-win" (cup of murder). In view of such outrage against virtue, chastity, and Christianity, Pokagon can not and will not hold "nin-o-daw-naw" (his tongue), but must cry out for all good men and women everywhere to put forth all their powers to crush out the deadly "kot-agis-iwin" (plague) and dry up the awful stream of misery and "gi-nib-owin" (death) at its fountainhead. There are in these United States not more than one-half million of people engaged in the sale of this curse, and yet to those comparative few, "nin-misk-wing-we-see" (I blush) to say it, millions, politicians and statesmen, all alike bow down and worship at their shrine, as if they held eternal rewards and punishments in "on-ina-gi-maw-og" (their hands). A small "a-nack-wad" (cloud) may hide "mi-chi kis-sis" (the mighty sun) from view at noonday, one hand may shut from sight the glittering vault of "waw-kwi" (heaven) at "a-bit-a-tib-e kad" (midnight); so some little selfish interest, if unchecked, may "ni-bo" (eclipse) the most righteous cause on earth. In conclusion, permit me to say, although by nature I am a child of "saw-kaw" (the forest), and was born "O-gimaw" (Chief), yet, by adoption, I am a citizen of the United States, having the right of petition, therefore take the liberty to say to white men everywhere, who now occupy this loved land of my fathers and mothers, "Ki-mo-kas!" (Come forth!) "In-aw-bi-win gi-wit-tai!" (Do look about you!) "Wi-i-a-gad sa-gid-i-win" (Pity and love), with outstretched "on-i-kag" (arms), are emploring you to save the perishing. Some one's loved Olondaw is staggering to a drunkard's "tchi-be-gamig" (grave). Some one's loved Hazeleye is being pushed by drunken men into "sa-gi-a-gan nib-o-win" (the lake of death) without a hand to save. Some one's dear, loved Lonidaw is weeping over them, dying "maw-kish-ka o-daw-win" (broken hearted). Somebody's Pokagon, robbed of wife and children, is lost and wandering in "maw-kaw-te mit-i-gag" (the dark woods) of despair, desolate and alone, tonight.

If you will not try to console and help them, do not I beg and pray of you, be less humane than savages or beasts of prey that always fight for and protect "win-osh-ki" (their young) of tender age. Somebody's little children are crying all about you in rags and want because of the curse of "ish-kote-wabo" (rum). Do, I beg of you, draw them near unto "ki kaki-gan" (your breast), and awaken in "kin o-daw" (your hearts) if possible, though feeble it may be, the mother's love as she draws the nursing infant to *her* breast to hush its sobs and dry "nin-maw" (its tears), and then tell Pokagon if you will not volunteer to march under "me-no ki-ki-weon" (the noble flag) of total abstinence, that it may finally, in triumph, float from sea to sea, and from the Gulf to the Great Lakes. It can and must be done. The Supreme Court of these United States has declared the use of intoxicating drinks a nuisance, and that laws for its suppression are proper and legal, yet strange to say, many who advocate the sale of it, and some who claim they are good and true temperance men and women, answer: "Yes, we believe and will admit all that the Supreme Court has declared; but also believe such laws would be a dead letter on our statute books unless the people are educated to a standard as high as the law itself." All must admit that if we should "nib-waw-kaw'-win" (reason) from such analogy, we would come to "deb-we-tam-win" (the conclusion) that no laws are necessary, but simply education. Pokagon believes if that time ever does dawn upon human nature, it will be when the golden rule is born in every heart, and every one shall love his neighbor as himself, and our seventy millions of people shall possess the true character of Christ. Then, and not until then, can any people prosper without proper laws to restrain them. A few years since, as I passed through the peach belt of southwestern Michigan, I noticed in many of the peach orchards along my route men were at work digging up the trees, root and branch, and burning them. I also observed that many of the trees were loaded with ripe fruit of red and crimson intermixed, tempting to behold, which were also burned with them. I made careful inquiry for the cause of such wanton destruction, and was told the trees were diseased with a contagion known as the "yellows," and that the charming ripe fruit I had seen was premature and diseased, and that it was known among fruit growers as "mock peaches," and further, that the State of Michigan had decreed that all such diseased trees must be destroyed; and if the orchard owners neglected to do so, the State of Michigan would destroy them at the owner's expense, and subject them to the payment of a fine of one hundred dollars in each case, and imprisonment if not paid. Today I passed over the same route again; and where eight years ago the land was cursed with dying trees and mock peaches, I beheld spread out before me in every direction, beautiful orchards loaded with rich, ripe fruit, red-cheeked, and in the bloom of health, which, in contrast with the dark-green foliage of the trees, presented a living picture which excited "nin-o-daw" (my heart) to cry out, "Behold Eden's garden of the nineteenth century." Men, women, and children with jest and jeer, with laugh and merry song on every hand, were picking and packing the fruit, while others, with teams were hauling it away, some to the railroad, and some to the lake for shipment, while the employed and the employer were happy alike, and rejoiced together.

Now let Pokagon ask, in all candor. What brought about this mighty change from "kot-a'-git-o'-win" (adversity) to "jaw-end-a'-gos-i'-win" (prosperity), from "gi-nib-owin" (death) unto "bim-adis-iwin" (life)? But one answer can be truly given, "The State of Michigan did it." With a single blow of her right "o-nik" (arm) she crushed the wide-spread contagion, and yet there are many who still dare say, unblushingly, in both private and public life in the face of such convincing facts, and thousands of like cases, "that no law can be enforced to prohibit the sale and manufacture of intoxicating drinks."

My native "nin-dib" (brains) are indeed puzzled to understand how it is that the incoming white race, by their intelligence and skill, have invented instruments whereby they can measure "waw-kwing" (the heavens) above, and declare of what substance "an-ang-ong" (the stars) are composed; who have provided means whereby they can travel at ease in palaces, sweeping above "se-ben-og" (rivers), and through "wad-jog" (mountains), outstripping, in their course, the flight of birds in their migration; who have provided means whereby they can enjoy parlor life while crossing oceans in the teeth of the wildest "no-din-og" (storms); who have perfected inventions whereby they can rise above "mi-gi-si" (the eagle) in his flight, or descend into the depths of the sea where fish can scarcely swim; whose subtle brains have devised means whereby they can talk as though face to face, around the globe; whose ingenuity can successfully bottle up "gi-git-iwin" (speech) whereby generations yet unborn may listen to the voices of their forefathers; from whose brains eminated that marvelous invention by means of which a button pressed by the fingers of a child, causing mountains to be rent asunder and torn down, or the granite bottom of the sea uplifted and broken in pieces. All those wonderful achievements the white men have accomplished, and yet they dare have the effrontery to declare to all the world by words and deeds, regardless of their marvelous works almost divine, that they are not able to provide means whereby they can destroy "tchi maw-tchi gi-go" (that great devil-fish) which their own hands have fashioned and launched upon the sea of human life, whose tenticles reach out to do their wicked work alike into wigwams and palaces, into schools and colleges, into halls of legislation and courts of law, and all unsought, crushes in its coils the heart of the young bride, the wife, the mother, and the little child. Now if it be true the dominant race lack the power to bind down and destroy that monstrosity born of their own race, then it must also be true that the moral science of good government, for the best good of all the people, has not kept pace with their remarkable discoveries and improvements. At this very time some of the best "wi-yi-tip" (brains) of our country are laboring night and day to provide instruments whereby the seed of disease, or any foreign substance, may be seen in the human body to aid surgery in relieving the afflicted.

The people are wildly clapping their hands over it, and "bi-ba-gi-win" (shouting) loud acclaim, and yet these benevolent men of "win-di-go" (giant) research and their votaries, as well as many of our political and moral scientists, can not or will not see "pa-ga-ka-ban" (in broad daylight) the curse of the glass between "odon" (the lips) of our boys and young men who are rushing down the toboggan-slide of shame into the broad gateway of physical ruin and moral death.

It is well for the agriculturist to study chemistry, that he may understand the property of the soil, and prepare it for the golden grain. But he who would so prepare his land and plant it with the best of seed, and then allow "mäsh-kos-sue" (the grass) and "maw-tchi-mash-kos-sue" (the noxious weeds) to choke out the young and tender plants, would be considered foolish with all his wisdom. Our "aki" (country) is one vast field for our cultivation; science, with a lavish hand, has given us ample means to dress and take care of it, and yet, to the shame of this nation, cigarette weeds, whisky weeds, and all manner of vicious weeds are running it over, demoralizing alike the young men and the little boys. Fathers and mothers, Pokagon asks you in the name of "o-gwis-si-mag" (the sons) of "saw-kaw" (the forest); he asks you in the name of "Ki-je-manito" (the Great Spirit) of his fathers and yours; in the name of "an-i-shin-äb-e-wi-win" (humanity) and Christianity, and by all that is sacred and dear to "an-ish-in-aw-be" (mankind), is it not your duty to destroy those deadly weeds "o-tchi-bik gaie wad-i-kwane" (root and branch)? Ancient and modern history, written and traditional, both declare most emphatically that in order to attain to the most perfect type of civilization for the best good of all, the people must be equally developed, morally, mentally, and physically. And yet it must appear to every candid-thinking man, as he beholds "min-ik-wesh-kiwin" (intemperance) sweeping our land like "mash-ko-de ish-ko-te" (a prairie on fire), scorching all that is fair and lovely, that the lack of moral education to map out proper legislation is the most lamentable defect of the present age.

XII

In the mighty onward march of research and improvement, Pokagon has no desire to tighten the reins, to curb physical or scientific development; but in driving the triple team that moves the great car of civilization, he would cautiously urge forward that one which lags behind, that all in concert might keep step side by side, until the goal is reached. The most humble prayer of Pokagon is that the great and learned who now occupy this loved land of his fathers and mothers, may in "ni'-ga-win" (the future) labor as zealously to search out the science of good government for the best good of all the people, as they have been in the past to search out the science of the physical world about them. Let knowledge and righteousness march shoulder to shoulder, onward and upward, until the mountain top is gained, where the perpetual sunshine of social purity will cleanse the hearts of all, breaking asunder the gauling chains of intemperance, letting the oppressed go "di-ben'-in-dis" (free). All along the seacoast of "nin aw-kee" (this land of ours), and along the shores of "tchi-i-gi-tchi-gami" (the great inland lakes) have been erected by the United States nearly three hundred life-saving stations, from whose watch towers a lookout is kept day and night to rescue ships and those on board. These stations are manned by thousands of stalwart men and experienced seamen, equipped with all the latest improvements of the life-saving service at the expense of millions of dollars annually. During the last fiscal year the general superintendent of this branch of service, in great pride, reports "that six hundred and thirteen shipwrecked lives were saved." That branch of service is indeed a noble one, and worthy the hearty approbation of all; and yet, as we reflect upon the limited opportunity it affords to save "bi-go-nesh-ka" (shipwrecked) humanity, as compared with that offered along the vast "kitch-i-gaw-me" (seashore) of "min-ik-esh-ki-win" (intemperance), whose tides and alluring waves sweep over and drown its hundreds of thousands every "bi-boon" (year),—in view of such wanton destruction, Pokagon in "nin-o-daw" (his heart) feels compelled to cry aloud to the present lawgivers of "nin-gaw aukee" (his fathers' land), Do extend your life-saving service to "mi-chi kitch i-gaw-me" (the great ocean) of struggling "nish-i-wan-a-dis" (humanity). Throw out "bim-a-dis-e-win bi-mina-kwan'" (the life-line) of total abstinence, and save the perishing! For nearly sixty years I have associated with "wau-be-au-ne-ne" (the white race) as well as my own, and by close observation during all that time, I am fully convinced that the only safe "ako-bim'-wan" (fortress) of "in-ini'-jimo-win" (refuge) against the ravages of "tchi-maw-tchi" (that curse) *is total abstinence.*

Disguise it as the pride of the white man may, his safest security, as well as ours, is in the absence of temptation. We are now in the midst of an exciting presidential campaign of 1896. One of the great political parties is clamoring with pen and tongue that "se-wan" (the money) in circulation is inadequate to meet the demands of the people; and that as a result the laboring classes are struggling under "na-bik-a-gan" (the yoke) of poverty in the midst of plenty, and that peace and prosperity can only be secured by opening the mints of the United States to the free and unlimited coinage of "jo-ni-ia" (silver); while the other great party is declaring just as vehemently, that the depression complained of is not for the want of more money, but for the lack of proper tariff reform to protect the farmers and open our mills to American labor. On these issues the two great parties are clamoring before the people night and day for the mastery at the polls. And O, how hard they toil and "ab-weso-win" (sweat) to secure men's votes! No "ke-ti-mesh-kig" (tramps) now beg from "ish-kwan-dem tchi ish-kwan-dem" (door to door); all are corralled and "ash-an-ge" (fed) for their votes until election day comes round.

No doubt both parties act from their honest convictions, each believing its own doctrine sound, and that if carried out, would bring peace and prosperity to the nation; but what most staggers Pokagon's "daw-naw-ki nib-waw'-kawin" (native reason) is how either party can hold its peace and not throw some responsibility for trying times for the laboring classes where it justly belongs, and openly condemn the manufacture of three billions of cigarettes which are consumed annually in this country by little boys and those of older years, at the expense of millions of dollars, receiving therefor only a deadly poison, want, disease, and premature death. The smoke of their torments blues the air, and is breathed in at every political club room in the land without reproof. And Pokagon is still more surprised that both of the great political parties do not cry out against that liquid fire of "nib-owin" (death) and "ana-mak-amig" (hell) that is "aki-gimosh-kaang-win" (deluging this land of ours) with poverty, shame, and crime, annually robbing the people of hundreds of millions of dollars for a damning curse that leads but to the grave.

In the stillness of the night, when wandering alone under the glittering canopy of heaven, asking in humility of prayer for "Kije-manito wa-kwi" (the God of heaven) to teach me if there is any reasonable excuse why partizans, politicians, and statesmen should not tread upon the neck of that soulless "maw-tchi" (tyrant) of humanity, my petitions have always been answered, but not in the voice of "ani-miki" (thunder), nor emblazoned in characters of living "ish-kote" (fire) across "waw-kwi" (the heavens), but in murmurs soft and low it has fallen upon "nin go-mo-win odaw" (my waiting heart) as gently as the dews of evening upon the grass and flowers, whispering in "nin tchi-tchang" (my soul), "Pokagon, there is no good excuse." Christian charity alone may try to cloak their nakedness by declaring to the world: They are so blinded by the love of party and so fearful of the liquor ballot they will not hear "ja-kaw-id" (the widow) and "wegi-mind" (the mother) pleading; they will not see the little child and "nin gi-wis'" (the orphan) weeping.

Again and again I am told it is an easy matter to find fault. And so it is; but not until "wabo-meme" (the dove) shall cease to cry out against "ke-kek" (the hawk) that steals and kills her young, will Pokagon cease to sound "mit-aw-haw-ho" (the war-whoop) of alarm against "nit-agan" (the destroyer) of your children and ours. But I do not wish to raise the hue and cry against the weakness of partizan spirit without offering a remedy for such frailties in human nature. I fully realize that most political leaders, as well as the rank and file of all parties, are equally anxious for good government, but honestly disagree what legislation will best secure it. Certainly, nearly all who are not financially connected with the accursed trade, and some who are, openly acknowledge that the use of it is a vice and a curse to any people, and that our nation would be far better off if it was struck from existence. Hence, in view of those facts, it can certainly be in some way wisely arranged between all political parties to have a like plank incorporated in the platform of each, clothed in such plain, simple language that even a child could not misunderstand it, declaring it to be their determination to crush out the deadly plague.

Go before the people with that vexed issue so disposed of in the platforms of all political parties, with only those issues to be brought before the people at the polls, on which they honestly disagree. Let this be done before the next presidential campaign, then each party can go before the people, pledged alike to the most sacred cause on earth; then that great fear of the liquor ballot, which so long has hung over the two great political parties like a funereal pall, will vanish as "tch-baw-i" (a phantom) of a nightly dream.

True it is the great cause of temperance ought never to have been "a-bin-od-ji" (an offspring) of one political party more than another.

It would be just as reasonable to make "bo-ta-do-win gaie me-no" (vice and virtue) a party issue as the cause of temperance; and yet it is no wonder that reformers, who, seeing such a gigantic evil slightly dealt with, should have joined heart and hand against it. As I stood in the cemetery near my home on last Decoration day, admiring the double line of girls and boys file right and left as they entered the gate following the soldiers' measured tread, placing fragrant flowers upon the star-spangled graves, I thought in my heart, How beautiful so to remember the honored dead, and teach our children loyalty by remembering those who fought to save the union; then my heart beat a second thought, and said, While we bring floral offerings for the soldiers and sailors of the Rebellion, let us not forget to place in tenderness the fairest flowers upon the graves of those noble men and women who against the curse of intemperance fighting fell—for God, for home, and native land. Yes, let us remember them, and teach our children to revere their names, and hallow each spot where the moral bold repose; but while we remember to honor the dead, let us not neglect to honor the living reformers also, and encourage *them*. Hark! Hear them calling for volunteers to stand in defense of the most righteous cause of suffering humanity! The God of your fathers and ours in heaven hears each pulsation of their loyal hearts, above the fife and beat of drum that calls for military glory. He, too, hears the liquor venders proudly boasting how they aid the poor by making annual payments of millions of dollars in taxes for the people. To them he openly declares, "It is written in the law of nin-o-daw (my heart) that he who stands most condemned of all before the bar of eternal justice is tchi ba-ta-do-dam (that sinner) who with one hand puts a dime into the urn of poverty, and with the other takes a dollar out."

In the darkest midnight of the Rebellion, when brave men began to fear the power of man, and the pious to doubt the favor of God, in response to a petition entitled "the prayer of twenty millions," Abraham Lincoln, as President of the United States, set at liberty three million slaves, and saved the union. Then why not now, in response to the prayer of more than forty millions, set at liberty millions—red, black, and white, bound hand and foot, while they kiss the rod of that despot,

King Alcohol. Come forth, all ye lovers of justice, equity, and humanity; stand in line, and in the name of your God, home, and country, move bravely forward under the glorious banner of Temperance, on which is emblazoned in characters of life, "Total Abstinence Now and Forever." Let the general government decree that noble emblem, royally begotten by pity and love, to be the law of this loved land of "nossog" and "nindaog" (my fathers and mothers); and Pokagon in full faith believes that, like the peach contagion of Michigan, in less than eight years King Cain of this generation will abdicate his throne forever, and the glorious "kesus" (sun) of universal temperance will roll away "a-nawk-wad-og" (the gloom-clouds) of sorrow and sadness that now hang like a funereal pall above us, and will shine forth in newness of life, while "naw-gwe-i-ab'" (the rainbow) of promise will hang its archway of cheering aspirations across the pathway of the departed storm, filling the hearts of weeping brides, mothers, and children everywhere throughout this glorious "au-kee" (land) of "nos-og" (my fathers) with great joy and gladness. "Tchi oshki-gijig" (That new day) of jubilee is surely coming; but on account of "aki-wesi" (old age) I do not expect to behold it; but, thanks to "waw-kwi" (high heaven), I am now permitted to stand where Moses stood, on the top of Mount Nebo, beholding "Gigig-win" (Paradise) regained, while from every future home in America I hear the welcome "inwe-win-og" (voices) of Pokagons and Lonidaws of every race with their loved children, shouting, "Victory! Victory!" which rolls on, undying, to freedom's farthest shores.

Appendix

From the many addresses delivered by Chief Pokagon, the following one has been selected by the publisher as appropriate for the "Queen of the Woods." It was delivered by the old veteran in the Gem Opera-house at Liberty, Ind., Jan. 7, 1898, under the auspices of Orinoco Tribe No. 184, I. O. R. M.

It was through the untiring efforts of Hon. E. E. Moore, of Ohio, that the chief was prevailed upon to leave his tribe, and travel over three hundred miles from home in midwinter to address that society.

The Address

For many years I have had a warm heart for the pale-faced Red Men, but never expected to be invited by them to deliver an address.

I would not have you think that I flatter myself that I have been invited here on account of my intelligence or reputation, as I most keenly realize that you have looked forward to my coming here with a sort of novel pride, that you might point me out to your children and say, "Behold a living specimen of the race with whom we once neighbored,—a race we sometimes loved, and yet that love was mingled with distrust and fear." No greater compliment could have been bestowed upon our vanishing race than by naming one of the grandest orders of America after them. And that compliment was made perpetual in giving each officer of the Red Men's Order Indian names pure and simple, as well as giving each lodge some appropriate Indian name. My heart is always made glad when I read of the Daughters of Pocahontas kindling their council fires. I have often thought that if they dressed as becomingly as our maids and matrons did in their native style, I would be glad indeed to see them confer the Pocahontas Degree work. The names Pocahontas and Pokagon (my own name) were derived from the same Algonquin word—"Po-ka"—meaning a "shield," or "protector." And again, we are highly complimented by the Order of Red Men in dating their official business from the time of the discovery of America. I suppose the reason for fixing that date was because our forefathers had held for untold ages before that time the American continent a profound secret from the white man. Again, the Red Men's Order highly compliments our race by dividing time into suns and moons, as our forefathers did, all of which goes to show that they understood the fact that we lived close to the Great Heart of Nature, and that we believed in one Great Spirit who created all things, and governs all.

Hence that noble motto, born with our race,—Freedom, Friendship, and Charity,—was wisely chosen for their guiding star. Yes, Freedom, Friendship, Charity! Those heaven-born principles shall never, never die! It was by those principles our fathers cared for the orphan and the unfortunate, without books without laws, without judges; for the Great Spirit had written his law in their hearts, which they obeyed.

Tradition, as sacred to us as holy writ, has taught us that our forefathers came to this country from the Atlantic coast. When they first entered these woodland plains, they said in their hearts, Surely we are on the border of the "happy hunting grounds" Beyond. Here they found game in great abundance. The elk, the buffalo, and the deer stood unalarmed before the hunter's bended bow. Fish swarmed the lakes and streams close to shore. Pigeons, ducks, and geese moved in great clouds through the air, flying so low that they fanned us with their wings; and our boys, whose bows were scarce terror to the crows, would often with their arrows shoot them down. Here we enjoyed ourselves in the lap of luxury.

But our camp-fires have all gone out. Our council fires blaze no more. Our wigwams and they who built them, with their children, have forever disappeared from this beautiful land, and I alone of all the chiefs am permitted to behold it again.

But what a change! Where cabins and wigwams once stood, now stand churches, schoolhouses, cottages, and castles. And where we walked or rode in single file along our winding trails, now locomotives scream like some beast of prey, rushing along their iron tracks, drawing after them long rows of palaces with travelers therein, outstripping the flight of eagles in their course.

As I behold this mighty change all over the face of this broad land, I feel about my heart as I did in childhood when I saw for the first time the rainbow spanning the cloud of the departed storm.

I do not speak of the past complainingly. I have always taught my people not to sigh for years long gone by, nor pass again over the bloody trails our fathers trod. I have stood all my life as a peacemaker between the white people and my own people. Without gun or bow I have stood between the two contending armies, receiving a thousand wounds from your people and my own. I have continued to pray the great father at Washington to deal justly with my people; and have said to my own people, when they were bitterly wronged, and felt mortally offended, "Wait, and pray for justice; the war-path will but lead you to the grave." At the beginning of the present century my father became chief of the Pokagon band. At that time the heroic Tecumseh with his great eloquence stirred up the Algonquin tribes to unite as one and strike for liberty. My father most emphatically declared they might as well attempt to stay a cyclone in its course as to beat back the on-marching hordes of civilization toward the setting sun. But in their loyal zeal they could not comprehend their own weakness and the strength of the dominant race, but being pressed onward by as noble motives as ever glowed in the breast of mortals, they fought most desperately for home and native land.

Historians have recorded of us that we are vindictive and cruel, because we fought like tigers when our homes were invaded, and we were being pushed toward the setting sun. When white men pillaged and burned our villages and slaughtered our families, they called it honorable warfare; but when we retaliated, they called it butchery and murder. When the white man's renowned statesman, Patrick Henry, proclaimed in the ears of the English colonies, "Give me liberty, or give me death," he was applauded by his people, and that applause still rolls on undying to freedom's farthest shores. When William Tell pierced the apple on the head of his son, Gessler noticed a second arrow drop from his vest. In tones of thunder he demanded, "Slave! why didst thou conceal that arrow?" Quick as lightning came the proud response, "To shoot thee, tyrant, if I had harmed my son." And all the civilized world, since then, through the centuries of time, have continued to applaud that sentiment. But let Pokagon ask, in all that is sacred and dear to mankind, why should the red man be measured by one standard, and the white man by another? The only answer I can give is that "mine" and "thine," the seed of all misery, predominate in the hearts of men when they become civilized and wealthy.

In conclusion, permit me to say, I rejoice with the joy of childhood that you have granted "a son of the forest" a right to speak to you; and the prayer of my heart, as long as I live, shall ever be that the Great Spirit will bless you and your children, and that the generations yet unborn may learn to know that we are all brothers, and that there is but one fold, under one Shepherd, and the great God is the Father of all.

Pokagon was Engaged to Address a Remarkable Gathering

Occupying the first page of the Chicago Sunday *Tribune* of March 5, 1899, appears a picture of a model of the first Fort Dearborn, presented to the Chicago Historical Society by Charlotte W. Pitkin, with an elaborate description of the same. It appears from this very interesting article that the late Edward G. Mason, formerly president of the society, had made arrangements when the model was formerly presented, to hold a great Fort Dearborn meeting at the rooms of the Historical Society building. A special car was to be provided to bring Mrs. Susan Winans, of California, who was born in the fort in 1812, to be present, and relate what her mother had told her about the fort and the massacre. The venerable Pokagon had been engaged to address the meeting, and give the Indian side of the massacre, as it had been told to him by his father and others, who were present. But owing to the death of the president and the late Chief Pokagon, the contemplated meeting was cancelled, and the model was presented without special program.

Pokagon's Death

While the foregoing romance of real life was being put in type, its author, Chief Pokagon, apparently in good health, suddenly died of pneumonia, Jan. 27, 1899. But the manuscript was completed, and the preface nearly written.

At the time of his death, he was much interested in making arrangements to go out on a lecturing tour, and make sale of his "Queen of the Woods" through northern Indiana, from whence his people, the Pottawattamies, were expelled in 1838 by order of Governor Wallace of that State, who was incited by false reports of avaricious white settlers who coveted the rich lands of the reservations.

Although Pokagon was but a boy eight years old at the time, yet the sting of the great injustice done his people so wounded his sensitive nature that he always tried to evade speaking of the cruel affair; and when pressed to do so, he would always say: "The authorities at Washington meant all right, but were deceived by bad agents who made them false reports, claiming the Indians had made the sacred cross to contracts which they had never signed, unless it was when they had been intoxicated through the influence brought to bear upon them by agents for that purpose."

Chief Simon Pokagon was a man of remarkable sturdy character, and highly honored by those who knew him best. He was unostentatious in manner, and of simple habits. He exhibited unrivaled patience and forbearance. When attacked by jealous enemies, he proceeded as though no unkindness was intended. He possessed the gift of retaining dates, names, and facts accurately in memory, and would never relax into commonplace conversation until all immediate business was satisfactorily completed. He was very fond of children, even playful with them; and much appreciated a good joke. He was in the habit of traveling long distances on foot, or otherwise, to attend to business connected with his people, and to make addresses where he was invited. In the death of this grand old chieftain the Indians have lost a most invaluable friend.

In Memoriam

A TRIBUTE TO THE MEMORY OF CHIEF SIMON POKAGON

BY LUELLA DOWD SMITH

The chief is dead; the strong and great—
The valiant brave of a valiant line—
A man Christ-led from the ways of hate
To the love forgiving, that is divine.

Two races mourn for the chief that is dead:
The forest braves of the dusky brow
And the pale-faced friends, together led
By a common grief, together bow.

In the loving words of their native speech,
"Kiji manito kaw-ki-naw," they said,
While our hearts made answer, each to each,
"We are brothers all, and our chief is dead."

Beyond Death's power is the realm of Life,
Where blossoms for aye the unfading flowers.
O "Queen of the Woods," O loving wife,
You shall find him there in the heavenly hours.

Like the leaves of the forest that fade and fall,
The Indian bands are passing by.
From the Spirit-land they hear the call,
Where their chief awaits in a home on high;

Where he waits in the blessed island of peace
Till the nations gather, no more at strife;
And sorrow and death forevermore cease,
Transformed in the waves of the river of life,

The river that circles the land of the blest.
Our Pilot has guided our chieftain across
To Ponemah, the home where the weary find rest,
And recompense comes for all of earth's loss.

Then march to the end with a strength that is brave,
Arising from sorrow and treading down sin.
The Lord of creation is strong to save,
And Christ is our Leader; at last we shall win.

A Tribute to Chief Simon Pokagon

May S. Wood,[1] a deep sympathizer with, and a devoted friend of, the late chief, expresses her affection for the Indian friend as follows:—

So thou art gone, my friend, my Indian father, from our sight;
Hast joined the throng of loved ones waiting There;
Hast heard the joyous "Welcome, chief and brother!"
From the multitudes of persecuted ones
Of thine own race, long since passed over.

---

1. May S. Wood, who is devoting her life to the Indian cause, has proved herself a staunch friend to Chief Simon Pokagon in soliciting aid for his last work, "Queen of the Wood;" also in making sale of birch bark and quill embroidery work of his people, and otherwise giving inspiration for the publication of his book. It was through the efforts of Mrs. Amelia Quinton president of the Woman's National Indian Rights Association, that aid was furnished the old chief by that society, to rebuild his home after it was destroyed by fire during the winter of 1898.—PUBLISHER.

Perhaps thy work was done, since so complete
Was every stroke of thine.
Yet such an one as thou could see no final end
To labor universal. For humanity's great cause engaged thy heart.

Among Earth's rarest minds we rank thy memory,
Though clothed in such simplicity of form and mien
As almost hidden was the burning soul within,
Save for the eloquence of truth so freely told.

No farewell do I say to thee, great benefactor ours;
Thou hast but stepped Beyond—out into Freedom.
Still we love and honor thee; still pursue
The course which thou inspired;

Knowing soon the fleeting years will bear us
To the same fair clime where thou and thine
And all the pale friends of thy race are gathered
Evermore.

—MAY S. WOOD
Feb. 6, 1899

(From the Hartford (Mich.) *Day-Spring.*)

Pokagon Honored

Mrs. H. H. Haynes, of Chicago, has interested herself in a burial-place for Chief Simon Pokagon, and the erection of a monument to his memory, to be paid for by the contributions of school children throughout the country. The following letter from the president of Graceland Cemetery has been forwarded to C.H. Engle, Esq.:—

GRACELAND CEMETERY COMPANY,
CHICAGO, Feb. 6, 1899

Mrs. H. H. Haynes,

5832 Jefferson Ave., Chicago

DEAR MADAM
     The Graceland Cemetery Company has selected a spot which seems an appropriate place for the burial of the Indian

Chief Pokagon, and if you can arrange for the removal of the remains to Graceland, the Cemetery Company will make no charge for the interment.

If you also succeed in getting subscriptions for a monument to the old chief, we should be glad to be consulted as to design of such a monument.

Very respectfully yours,
BRYAN LATHROP,
President

(From the Inter Ocean, March 16, 1899.)

The Pokagon Monument

The last hereditary chief of the Pottawattamies having died a few weeks ago, an organization has been formed in Chicago to erect a monument to his memory and to that of his father, Pokagon I, who was the great chief of the Pottawattamies during the days of the second Fort Dearborn and early Chicago.

The only memory left for coming generations of this race is the beautiful monument erected by the late Mr. George M. Pullman on the site of the massacre of the first fort's days.

The new Indian monument will be erected in Jackson Park, where throngs of visitors may become as familiar with its story as they are with that of the Massacre Monument.

The new monument will be erected in memory of the late Simon Pokagon, and will have inscribed upon it his own beautiful words to the children of Chicago, that "the red man and white man are brothers, and God is the Father of all."

Surmounting the pedestal will be a superb statue of the regal figure of Pokagon I in full chieftain's attire. The four bas-reliefs on the pedestal will represent events in the history of Chicago's Indian days, which will be decided upon by a committee of pioneers. The names, also, of noted Pottawattamie chiefs who were at the head of bands under Pokagon will be inscribed upon the base of the monument.

None of the children of today and very few of the grown people know that many of Chicago's suburbs and localities owe their names to the Indian chief who once lived on that very spot. The name of "Wilmette" may be found on the list, and that of many others.

It is the wish of the few pioneers left that the closing hour on some one of Chicago's school days every autumn may be set aside for Indian study, and called Pokagon Day; and that the children may learn from the old people to sing the weird cadences of the Indian songs, and to learn the beauty of that complicated language.

The Pottawattamies were a tribe of the great Algonquin family.

The Pokagon Monument Association numbers for its advisory committee and patrons the leading pioneers and prominent ladies and gentlemen of the city. The officers and executive committee will be chosen from among the children of the various sections of the city and suburbs.

A book containing the names of those who contributed to the monument will be placed in the library of the Chicago Historical Society.

THE FOLLOWING INDIAN LULLABY WAS found among the late chief's papers, supposed to have been written by request of Mrs. H. H. Hayes, of Chicago, to be sung at the "Concert of Cradle Songs of Many Nations" in one of the schools of the city:—

> *"O, close your bright eyes, brown child of the forest,*
> *And enter the dreamland, for you're tired of play;*
> *Draw down the dark curtain with long, silken fringes;*
> *Au-na-moosh*[2] *will attend on your mystical way.*

CHORUS:

> *"Hush-a-by, rock-a-by, brown little pappoose,*
> *O, can you not see, if you give the alarm?*
> *Zowan*[3] *beside you, is willing and eager*
> *To guard and defend you, and keep you from harm?*

> *"Wind-rocked and fur-lined, covered o'er with bright blanket,*
> *Your cradle is swung 'neath the wide-spreading trees,*
> *Where the singing of birds and chatting of squirrels*
> *Will lull you to rest midst the hum of wild bees.*

---

2. Dog.
3. Name of the dog.

Chorus.

"Your father is hunting to bring home the bear-skin,
While mother plaits baskets of various hue;
Na-co-mis[4] is weaving large mats of wild rushes,
And Nonnee sends arrows so swift and so true."

Chorus.

The last literary effort of the old veteran, so far as known, was in writing an Indian song by request of Chicago parties, which will more fully appear in the following article:—

(From the Daily *Inter Ocean*, Jan. 23, 1899.)

Chief Pokagon's Song

POTTAWATTAMIE LEADER WRITES IT FOR CHICAGO SCHOLARS— "QUEEN OF THE WOOD"—SANG AT A CONCERT GIVEN BY THE RAY AND JACKSON PARK SCHOOLS—HON. FERNANDO JONES, WHO PLAYED WITH THE INDIAN POET WHEN A BOY, SINGS HIS VERSE IN THE POTTAWATTAMIE LANGUAGE.

The early days of Chicago were brought back in vivid colors at the concert given by the children of the Ray and Jackson Park schools last Friday evening. One of the numbers was the singing of a song written for the occasion by Pokagon, chief of the Pottawattamies, followed by the singing of a genuine Pottawattamie song in the Indian language by Hon. Fernando Jones, vice-president of the Pioneers' Society.

The concert was given in the large assembly hall of the Hyde Park High School, which was filled to the doors. On the stage were over two hundred children in the costumes of the various important nations of the world. Each group, representing a certain nationality, sang in the language of the people of that country. In preparing for their part of the entertainment the little band to represent the American Indians wrote to Pokagon, whose father was chief of the Pottawattamies when Chicago

---

4. Grandmother.

was a government military station, requesting that he write a song for them to sing on this occasion. The learned Indian chief replied graciously with a pretty little legend in verse, entitled "Queen of the Wood."

The children were delighted with the honor of introducing to the public a song that will become a part of the history of Chicago, and entered into the task of learning it with unwonted zest. At the concert, one little "Indian maid," in costume, sang the solo, and the others joined in the refrain. The song follows:—

"QUEEN OF THE WOOD."

Now, listen, dear children, I've much I would tell you
Of a dusky-eyed maid long, long ago,
To whom squirrels would chat in the best way they could,
And hail the dear maiden as "Queen of the Wood."

CHORUS:

Queen of the Wood, Queen of the Wood!
All hail! all hail! Queen of the Wood!

The flowers looked up and smiled when she passed,
And joined with the birds in the songs which they sung;
And wherever she went in her sunshiny mood,
The children all hailed her as "Queen of the Wood."

CHORUS.

As she skimmed o'er the lake in her birchen canoe,
Her deer white as snow, on the shore trail would follow,
As she sang the sweet songs of the days of childhood,
While the winds and waves murmured, "Queen of the Wood."

CHORUS.

In the wild rose and dewdrops no jewels she lacked;
And full well she knew where the red-berries grew.
I wooed and I won this fair maid so kind and good,
And Pokagon's bride was then "Queen of the Wood."

Chorus.

At the conclusion of the song by the children, Hon. Fernando Jones, who, in his boyhood, knew Pokagon and his father, appeared in Indian costume, and, after telling the audience much of interest on the subject of Chicago's Indian music, he sang the song written by Pokagon, in the language of the Pottawattamies. The following is the legend in the original:—

> *Non-gom pe-sin-dem a-bi-nong nin ne-bi-naw*
> *Dib-adg-im-ki maw-kaw-te-wis i-kwe waw-gin weng,*
> *Au-saw-nawg-gog in-en-dawn gi-git me-no-ki*
> *Gaush-ki-ton, "Hoi, i-kwe; O-gi-maw-kwe Mit-i-gwa-ki!"*
> *"O gi-maw-kwe Mit-i-gwa-ki!" Hoi, "O-gi-maw-kwe*
> *Mit-i-gwa-ki."*

> *Waw-bi-gon-og daw-ta-gaw-nab baw-pi-win*
> *Taw-pe-ki kaw-bi-kawn nin maw-mawn i-ton,*
> *Mi-ne-she naw-gaw-man mi-se-mise-we*
> *Nin saw-gaw-am-ki Ke-sus-win mi-kawn sa;*
> *"Hoi, wis-kon-ge." O-gi-maw-kwe Mit-i-gwa-ki!*
> *"O-gi-maw-kwe Mit-i-gwa-ki! Hoi, O-gi-maw-kwe Mit-i-gwa-ki!"*

The Pottawattamie version is the first song in that language ever printed or sung in the city. Many of Chicago's old pioneers (now millionaires), when children, had the little Indians for their playmates, and each could speak the other's language as easily as he could speak his own.

Pokagon is nearly seventy years old. He is the son of the chief who was early Chicago's "Pokagon, chief of the Pottawattamies."

Simon Pokagon was educated for a priest, and speaks five languages. He is still living near Hartford, Mich., and is the only living son of Leopold Pokagon, having been born at Pokagon village in 1830. He has the distinction of being the best educated and most distinguished full-blooded Indian probably in America. He has written much and delivered many addresses of real literary merit during the past quarter of a century. He managed with consummate skill and ability the band of about three hundred Pottawattamies, of which he has for many years been the acknowledged head. His portrait was painted last September for Mr. Edward E. Ayer, president of the Field Columbian Museum, by the artist, Burbank, who felt the importance of Pokagon's latest book, the one telling of Chicago's early days, from stories told the son by his father, the elder Pokagon. Burbank urged the old chief to hurry, and gave him no peace until he got the book under way. It is now finished, and Pokagon is going to add this song to it in honor of Chicago's school children.

(From the Sunday *Inter Ocean*, Jan. 29, 1899.)

Chief Pokagon Dies

LAST OF THE POTTAWATTAMIE RULERS PASSES AWAY—MAN OF DEEP WISDOM—ALEXANDER BEAUBIEN TALKS OF TWO ILLUSTRIOUS CHIEFS—POET'S USEFUL LIFE—DEAD LEADER OF THE POTTAWATTAMIES A LITERARY MAN—"QUEEN OF THE WOOD," PUBLISHED FIRST IN THE INTER OCEAN, IS REPRINTED.

Chief Simon Pokagon, who died Friday near Allegan, Mich., made a number of friends in Chicago during the World's Fair. He came to represent his tribe, and met many pioneers who had known his father. Among these were Hon. Fernando Jones and Alexander Beaubien. They had made friends with the old Pokagon, who maintained most friendly relations with the new settlers, and who frequently made the journey on foot from the Michigan reservation to Fort Dearborn to transact the business of his people. His son succeeded him at his death, assuming both the name and title of the chief who had won the respect of the white men.

"When my father was in the employment of John Jacob Astor, I often saw old Chief Pokagon," said Mr. Beaubien. "The government paid the Indians their annuity at Fort Dearborn, and whenever Pokagon came to Chicago, he would stop over some time. He was always a guest of my father, and in this way I came to know him. Although a boy at the time, I was greatly interested in him and his tribe, and anything he said or did was important to me. As I remember him, he was the best of Indians. He was honest, industrious, and religious. He had many friends, and was much loved by his tribe. He was a good Catholic, and both my mother and myself were baptized by the priest old Pokagon accepted as his adviser.

EFFECT OF HIS RELIGION

"In 1836 the government stopped paying the Indians at Fort Dearborn; in fact, they were driven away from this territory. Their reservation was changed to the one they occupied later at Paw Paw Grove, Ogle County, this State. Most of the Indians left for that territory, but old Pokagon and his followers held their ground in Michigan and stayed there. It was their religion that kept them there, and caused them to separate from their fellows."

Chief Simon Pokagon was the son of Chief Leopold Pokagon, who had been baptized by the Jesuit fathers. He was born at Pokagon village, near Niles, Mich., in 1830. He had the distinction of being the best educated full-blooded Indian in America. He wrote much and well, and delivered many addresses of considerable literary merit. He leaves behind him among the Indians no successor to his poetic and literary ability. He was educated for a priest, and spoke four languages. When his history shall be written, his name will be placed among the greatest men of the once powerful tribe of the Pottawattamies. Pokagon leaves a widow, who, like himself, is very intelligent. She lives at Hartford, Mich., where the family have resided for many years, and where their son, who had become a prominent citizen of the town, died a few weeks ago, leaving four young children, the two oldest of whom, a boy and a girl, are being educated at the government Indian school at Lawrence, Kan.

The poet chief managed with consummate ability and skill the often conflicting and delicate interests and affairs of the band of three hundred Pottawattamie Indians scattered over the State of Michigan Gifted with a fine education, and inspired by enlightened views, he was an instrument of far-reaching good to all his people.

VISITS TO NATIONAL CAPITAL

Chief Pokagon visited Washington several times during the administrations of Abraham Lincoln and General Grant, in the interest of his band, to procure payment from the government of several hundred thousand dollars due his people from the sale of over a million acres of land, including the present site of Chicago, which his father sold to the United States in 1833. He recently secured from the Federal government an appropriation of $150,000. He was the guest of Chicago during Chicago week of the World's Fair, and was the central figure on the great Chicago day of that week, owing to the fact that he was the son of the very chief who had once owned the city site, and transferred it to the United States. He rang, in the morning of that day, the new Liberty bell, after which he addressed the assembled thousands in behalf of his people. At the close of his address a grand rush was made for the old man by the eager crowd, with whom he shook hands until his arms gave out.

Several of Chicago's millionaires were once his playmates. Hon. Fernando Jones, vice-president of the Pioneer Society, and who played with the Indian poet when a boy, was present at an entertainment given a week ago at the Hyde Park School, and told the audience a number of anecdotes and incidents connected with Pokagon and his father. The last literary work done by Pokagon was a poem written for this entertainment, and entitled "The Queen of the Wood." The poem was sung by the children on that occasion, Mr. Jones rendering the Pottawattamie version of the song. The Pottawattamie manuscript of the song is in the possession of Mrs. H. II. Hayes, of No. 5832 Jefferson Ave., and will be presented by her to the Chicago Historical Society, to be preserved for coming generations.

Within the past five years Chief Pokagon addressed many pioneer meetings in Indiana and Michigan, always attracting large crowds. He wrote many articles of real merit, which have been published in such leading magazines as the *Arena, Forum, Harper's, Chautauquan,* and *American Review of Reviews.* His "Red Man's Greeting," which was published during the spring of the World's Fair in a booklet made of manifold birch bark, was termed by Professor Swing the "Redman's Book of Lamentations." He has been termed by the press the "Longfellow of his race."

The last poem written by Pokagon, both in its English and Indian versions, appeared in the *Inter Ocean* last Monday, and is the only Pottawattamie song in the Pottawattamie language that has ever appeared in print.

(This poem may be found on page 236 of this book.—Publisher.)

(From the Chicago *Times-Herald*, Jan. 28, 1899)

Pokagon is Dead

AGED INDIAN CHIEF EXPIRES NEAR ALLEGAN, MICH.—SON OF A NOTED POTTAWATTAMIE, HE BECAME THE LEADER AND FATHER OF HIS BAND.

The death of Simon Pokagon occurred this morning at his home in Lee Township, Allegan County.

It is supposed that he was born in 1825 near Bertrand, Mich., and was christened at Bertrand in 1829. During the past year he wrote a book on the Indian that will no doubt have a large sale. Although the dead chief was the master of four languages, his book is written in that eloquent yet simple style for which he was noted.

It was Simon Pokagon's father, Leopold Pokagon, who, in 1833, signed the treaty made by the Indians, whereby the site of Chicago came into possession of the white man.

An affecting picture is drawn by the historians of the period of the heart-breaking reluctance with which the Indians took their departure from the St. Joseph Valley. Col. L. M. Taylor, of South Bend, accompanied Pokagon when he left his beautiful hunting-grounds, and he describes the occasion as one of the deepest sorrow to the Indians.

The chiefs had been sacredly enjoined by their people not to sign away their rights to the lands. But under the influence of the government agents, whisky and bribery did their work, and all but Pokagon signed the treaty. A little later, Colonel Taylor induced Pokagon to sign; but as the old chief took up the pen and walked to the table to do so, hot tears ran down his dusky cheeks and upon his buckskin jacket, and he said: "I would rather die than do this." In 1836 Pokagon and his whole band left their old home, and the red man was never seen there again.

(From the Chicago *Tribune*, Jan. 28, 1899.)

Death of Simon Pokagon

AGED CHIEF OF THE POTTAWATTAMIES PASSES AWAY

The death of Simon Pokagon took place this morning near Allegan, Mich.

It was Leopold Pokagon, his father, who, in 1833, signed the treaty made by the Indians whereby Chicago came in possession of the white man.

Chief Pokagon spent many of the best years of his life in trying to collect from the government the Pottawattamie claim of over $150,000, and two years ago the claim was paid. It was Pokagon's wish that he could live to see his people receive this money, and in this he was gratified.

The attention given the chief at the World's Fair in 1893 would have turned many a white man's head, but Pokagon returned to his people with an idea that his tribe might yet be made better. When the government turned over the immense amount of money to the tribe two years ago, the chief called his men together, and tried to instil in their minds the necessity of building homes and raising crops.

Pokagon has but one son, Charles, who aspires to rank first with the tribe. His wife is but fifty years of age, and from her appearance has shared but little of the old chieftain's troubles.

The chief in his life made frequent trips to the government schools at Lawrence, Kan., and through his efforts secured admittance for many of the children of the Pottawattamie tribe. Some of the graduates from this school give the chief the credit of their education.

It is conceded by the men of this city with whom the chief has transacted business for twenty-five years that had he been given the advantages of the race that imposed upon him, he would have been a leader among the bright intellects of today.

(From the Chicago *Evening Post*, Jan. 28. 1899.)

Knew Chief Pokagon

ALEXANDER BEAUBIEN TALKS OF DEAD POTTAWATTAMIE LEADER—HE ALWAYS WAS A GOOD INDIAN—WORKED FAITHFULLY TO CONSERVE THE INTERESTS OF HIS PEOPLE—WAS FRIENDLY TO THE WHITES.

The death of Chief Simon Pokagon of the Pottawattamie Indians, reported late yesterday from Holland, Mich., was received with deep regret in Chicago, where the old chief had many friends and acquaintances. Some few of his old friends are still living, among them being Hon. Fernando Jones and Alexander Beaubien. Better known to these men than the chief who died yesterday, was his father, the old Chief Pokagon, who died several years ago. It was he who had to do with the early settlers of this city, and it also was he who, many times each year during the early pioneer days, would make the journey on foot from the Michigan reservation to Fort Dearborn to transact the business of the Indians with the government. His son succeeded him at his death in name and title, and only during the last five years of his life did he attempt to become acquainted with his father's old friends. Chief Pokagon was eighty years old, and was the last of the royal line in his tribe. He always had been a great power among his people, and was known in Chicago more by reputation than personally.

KNEW POKAGON'S FATHER

"I did not know the late Chief Pokagon nearly so well as I did his father, the old chief, who died many years ago," said Mr. Beaubien today. "In the early days of this city, when my father was in the employ of John Jacob Astor, and kept a trading post as agent for the Northwestern American Fur Company, I saw old Chief Pokagon frequently. The government paid the Indians their annuity at Fort Dearborn, and Pokagon, whenever he came to Chicago, would stop over some time. He always was a guest of my father, and in this way I came to know him.

WORKED FOR HIS TRIBE

"The first I saw of the new chief, the man who died yesterday, was in 1893, the year of the World's Fair. He was here representing his tribe, and tried hard to get the mayor to appropriate a sum of money for a separate exhibition at the Fair. He called on me several times while in the city, and I found him a most agreeable and entertaining person. At first I was not fully convinced that he was Chief Pokagon, but when he had told a number of incidents relating to his father, which I remembered, I was convinced he was none other than the chief.

"His father was a good Indian, and so was he. He resembled his father in some ways, but did not have the same physique. I found on better acquaintance many of his father's lovable traits, and he was quite as fascinating to me as his father had been when I was a boy. After the Fair he returned to Michigan. I should imagine he lived much alone, and was not so fond of having much to do with others as his father had been. Three different times since the World's Fair year Pokagon has visited Chicago to my knowledge, and at each of these visits he spent his time with me at my house. So far as I know these visits were of a business nature, but he never said anything definite about his affairs. The last time he was here was in 1896."

NOTES A COINCIDENCE

Mr. Beaubien today celebrated the anniversary of his seventy-seventh birthday. The death of Chief Pokagon to him was a great surprise, and quite a coincidence that the son of his father's old friend should die on the eve of the anniversary of Mr. Beaubien's birthday. The two were nearly the same age. Mr. Beaubien was born seventy-seven years ago in a log cabin in the neighborhood of old Fort Dearborn, the site of this cabin being at present just east of Michigan Avenue, between Washington and Randolph Streets. The Beaubien family is recognized as the original founders of Chicago—the second Chicago after the great massacre. Mr. Beaubien claims to be the first white child born in this place.

(From the Chicago Record, Jan. 28, 1899.)

Chief Simon Pokagon Dead

HEAD OF THE POTTAWATTAMIE INDIANS EXPIRES
AT HIS HOME IN MICHIGAN

Old Chief Simon Pokagon of the Pottawattamie Indians, died at his home in Lee Township, Allegan County, today. He was nearly eighty years old, and the last of the line of royalty in his tribe. He was born in Pokagon, near Niles, Mich. He had always been a power for good among his people, recently securing for them $150,000 annuity due from the government, but many years in arrears. He visited President Lincoln soon after his inauguration, being the first Indian ever in the White House; and interviewed General Grant there in 1874. He had an enviable reputation as a public speaker, his sentiments being pathetic, and his addresses betraying kindness of heart and earnestness of thought. He was engaged when death claimed him in writing the Indians' side of the Fort Dearborn massacre, which he claimed had always been misrepresented. He was also pushing a claim for a large tract of land in the heart of Chicago, which he claimed belonged to his tribe.

An Interesting Document

The recent death of Pokagon has induced Samuel H. Row, of Lansing, Mich., to furnish for publication a document, of which the following is a copy:—

> Proceedings of a council held at the Cary Mission, St. Joseph, between the officers of Third Brigade Michigan militia and the head chiefs and warriors of the Pottawattamie Nation, on Sunday, the 27th day of May, 1832.
>
> After the council was opened and the object of it explained by Colonel J. Stewart, subagent, Brigadier-General Brown, after some conversation with the Indians relating to the hostile Sacs and Kickapoos, proceeded to ask the following questions:—
>
> *Question.*—What object had the Pottawattamies in view in the councils lately held by them?
>
> *Answer.*—The object of our council here was to instil into our families the principles of religion and temperance. We sent deputies to Nottawasepi and to the Ottawas to hold council on the same subject.
>
> *Q.*—Are Topenabee, Pokagon, or any of the chiefs professors of religion?
>
> *A. by Pokagon.*—[5]I am a professor of religion, and anxious for all my brethren to join me; and am anxious to be at peace with all men.
>
> *Q.*—Why have the Pottawattamies not planted corn at Nottawasepi this year?

---

5. The Pokagon referred to in this conversation was Leopold, the first of whom we have any history, and father of Simon, recently deceased.

A. by Pokagon.—They drink too much. I sent them word to quit drinking and plant corn, and live like white people. Everybody knows me, and knows Pokagon won't lie.

Q.—Do you know that the Sacs and Kickapoos are at war with the whites, and have murdered a number of families?

A. by Pokagon.—We have heard they were at war, but have heard but little about it.

Q.—Do you think yourselves able to protect yourselves and families against the Sacs and Kickapoos, should the whites remain at home, and the Sacs and Kickapoos come through your country?

A. by Pokagon.—Here are the men of this reserve; you see them all. We can't protect ourselves; we can't go to war; but if they come here, we will defend ourselves.

Q.—Should your services be required, would you be willing to send some of your young men with the American army to fight the Sacs and Kickapoos?

A. by Pokagon.—We are willing to send some of our young men should you want them.

General Brown assured them that while they remained at peace they should be protected the same as the whites. "The president and governor are your fathers, and they will protect your children."

Pokagon spoke and said: "We are glad that our fathers will protect us, and I believe that there is but one God, and that we are all brothers. I wish to remain at peace. I see no pleasure except in clothing my children and tilling my ground."

JACOB BEESON,
Brigade Quartermaster, Third Brigade, Michigan Militia, and Acting Aide-de-camp.
GEORGE W. HOFFMAN, *Acting Adj. Reg. M. M.*
JOSEPH BERTRAND, *Interpreter*

The council was held in a grove near the mission, about a mile distant from Niles, the present headquarters of the Third Brigade of Michigan Militia.

From the good feeling evinced by the Indians, and their answers and remarks, all were of opinion that their friendship could be relied upon, and that confidence can be placed in them. At the close a number volunteered their services to accompany the militia West, should they be invited.

JACOB BEESON,
GEORGE W. HOFFMAN

I hereby certify the within to be a true transcript of the proceedings had in the within-named council at Cary Mission, May 27, 1832.

E. R. CHAMPLAIN,
Aide-de-camp to Brig.-Gen. I. W. Brown,
Third Brigade Mich. Militia

(From the Chicago *Times-Herald,* Feb. 21, 1899.)

Pokagon Honored

CHIEF POKAGON'S NEW GRAVE

The body of Chief Simon Pokagon, the last of the Pottawattamie chiefs, who died near Allegan, Mich., Jan. 27, will be buried in Graceland Cemetery. Through the efforts of Mrs. H. H. Hayes, 5832 Jefferson Avenue, the Graceland Cemetery Company has donated the lot which is near the grave of John Kinzie, the first white resident of Chicago.

"The Red Man's Greeting"

A HAND-MADE BIRCH-BARK BOOKLET

This book will take its place in the cabinets of admirers of handsome books along with the carved leather bindings and illuminated text of the early German publishers; the heavy oaken-covered books of the first English works; the minute rice paper books of India; the stone tablets of the Phenicians, and the parchments of the Greeks, as the representative work of the nationality to which the author belonged. It abounds in all the rich metaphor and eloquence of the aboriginal race.

New York Globe

There is a bit of nature about it that seems to breathe the very air of some chieftain's home in the forest.

Detroit Sunday News

No words of mine can tell the pathos of this tiny book. From start to finish it seems to be a cry of anguish from the red man's heart. It is told simply, and yet with a force that leaves an indelible picture on your mind.

Teresa Dean, in Chicago Inter Ocean

It is a revelation of the Indians' poetry of thought, and in point of eloquence is excelled by nothing in the English language. Its source, character, and the uniqueness of its texture make it in truth a literary gem well worth the having.

Salem Herald-Advocate

In the *Arena* magazine of November, 1893, in a thorough review of "The Red Man's Greeting," by Mrs. Hattie Flower, of Boston, appears the following:—

This tiny booklet, called forth by our Columbian anniversary, is seasonable, and, in its rusticity, characteristic of a child of the forest. Printed upon white birch bark in its natural state is an account of the cruel betrayal of this hunted race, dating from the advent of the white man to these shores up to the present time. One reads with unutterable sadness this voicing of the outraged spirit of a race, eloquent in its pathos, yet entirely free from wild vindictiveness. The aborigines have ever been notable for their inborn poetic and oratorical powers. A bit of literature so clearly indicative of this phase of their nature is worthy of careful preservation.

In the July number of the aforesaid magazine is a lengthy illustrated review by the editor, B. O. Flower, in which appears the following:—

About the time of the opening of the Columbian Exposition, Chief Pokagon published a little booklet, entitled "The Red Man's Greeting," printed on the bark of the white birch tree.

This "Greeting" was pitched in a minor key. The plaintive note of the representative of a warrior race who had beheld the glory of his people vanish, characterizes it throughout. It is so entirely out of the ordinary in all particulars that I reproduce in this paper the author's preface, enlarged, and photographed from a leaf of the birch bark on which it is printed:—

PREFACE OF "THE RED MAN'S GREETING"

My object in publishing "The Red Man's Greeting" on the bark of the white birch tree, is out of loyalty to my own people, and gratitude to the Great Spirit, who, in his wisdom, provided for our use, for untold generations, this most remarkable tree with manifold bark, used by us instead of paper, being of greater value to us, as it could not be injured by sun or water. Out of the bark of this wonderful tree were made hats, caps, and dishes for domestic use, while our maidens tied with it the knot that sealed their marriage vow; wigwams were made of it, as well as large canoes that outrode the violent storms on lake and sea; it was also used for light and fuel at our war-dances and spirit-councils. Originally, the shores of our Northern lakes and streams were fringed with it and evergreen, and the white, charmingly contrasted with the green, mirrored from the water, was indeed beautiful; but, like the red man, this tree is vanishing from our forests.

> *"Alas for us! our day is o'er,*
> *Our fires are out from shore to shore;*
> *No more for us the wild deer bounds;*
> *The plow is on our hunting-grounds;*
> *The pale man's ax rings through our woods,*
> *The pale man's sails skim o'er our floods;*
> *Our pleasant springs are dry.*
> *Our children—look by power oppressed!—*
> *Beyond the mountains of the West,*
> *Our children go to die."*

ANY ONE DESIRING A COPY of this relic of the woods, can procure one by sending fifty cents to the publisher, C. H. ENGLE, Hartford, Mich.

Indian Skill in Splint and Bark Work

Below is subjoined an extract taken from two articles written by Chief Pokagon, one entitled "Our Indian Women," the other, "Indian Skill." The first appeared in the *Chautauquan* of March, 1896; the other, in the same magazine in February, 1898. The two articles have been read and reread with great interest:—

In winter time our girls and women are most industriously engaged in manufacturing splint baskets of mixed colors in all imaginable designs, varying in size from that of a lady's thimble to hampers holding two bushels or more. The women are quick to imitate and originate designs. Their finest work is made of white birch bark, sweet-grass, and porcupine quills. You can scarcely name an article of domestic use among the white people which they do not pattern after, such as tablemats, napkin-rings, watch cases, and even miniature houses and churches,—all fall from their fingers with equal skill. The porcupine quills are stained in all the colors of the rainbow. These they work into the bark of which the articles are made, representing various kinds of flowers with their leaves and branches in all their natural color.

Some tribes decorate with colored beads, but our women will use only such materials as they can get from nature's store, which speaks volumes for their ingenuity and originality. Sweet-grass is used on account of its fragrance, which it retains for many years.

This work of our women is much sought after by summer tourists. Indian women, as a general rule, have finely molded hands, and to watch the nimble fingers of those well skilled in the art is curiously interesting. Basket after basket is made in an incredibly short space of time, and packed away for sale or future use. In fact, no true admirer of the beautiful can look through a well-arranged collection of these goods without feeling in his heart that they must have been dipped in the rainbow and washed in the sunshine.

Out of the manifold bark of the white birch tree hats, caps, mats, boxes, and dishes are made for domestic use, as well as canoes of various sizes, and all kinds of devices to please and excite curiosity.

They also ornament their moccasins and native wearing apparel with various-colored porcupine quills, which gives a market value among us for an animal useless and despised by the white man. I do not speak of the skill of my race with a boastful heart, but because I most keenly realize that unless the natural ability of my people is recognized by the dominant race, they can not rise to that station which the God of nature entitles them.

Any one desiring to obtain specimens of this Indian work will address the *Pokagon family*, in care of *C. H. Engle*, Box 32, Hartford, Van Buren County, Mich.

A NOTE ABOUT THE AUTHOR

Simon Pokagon (1830–1899) was a Pokagon Potawatomi author and advocate. Born near Bertrand, Michigan Territory, he was the son of Potawatomi chief Leopold Pokagon. Educated at the University of Notre Dame and Oberlin College, he gained a reputation as an effective activist for the rights of indigenous peoples. Notably, he met with presidents Lincoln and Grant to petition for reparations from the government for violating the 1833 Treaty of Chicago, but was later accused of using his position to sell land to real estate speculators. Through his numerous articles, novels, stories, and poems, Pokagon became one of the first Native Americans to gain a national audience as a writer. In 1893, he was featured at the World's Columbian Exposition, where he spoke to a crowd of 75,000 on the dangers of alcoholism to Native Americans, citizenship, and unity. Pokagon's novel *O-gî-mäw-kwĕ Mit-i-gwä-ki* (1899) remains a landmark work of Native American literature.

A NOTE FROM THE PUBLISHER

bookfinity™

Discover more of your favorite classics with Bookfinity™.

- Track your reading with custom book lists.
- Get great book recommendations for your personalized Reader Type.
- Add reviews for your favorite books.
- AND MUCH MORE!

Visit **bookfinity.com** and take the fun Reader Type quiz to get started.

Enjoy our classic and modern companion pairings!

Printed in the USA
CPSIA information can be obtained
at www.ICGtesting.com
JSHW082348140824
68134JS00020B/1963

9 781513 283395